# A TRIO OF WORLDS

## BOOK ONE OF THE THREE WORLDS CHRONICLES

## JAMES R NORWOOD

KJN PUBLISHING

Copyright © 2021 James R Norwood

All rights reserved. No part of this work may be duplicated or used without prior written consent from the publisher.

ISBN: 978-0-578-90143-5
Published by KJN Publishing
https://www.threeworlds.net

*To Kelly, for believing in me and not thinking I was too crazy. I love you.*

BOOKS BY JAMES NORWOOD

- A Trio of Worlds: Book One of the Three Worlds Chronicles
- Heirs of the Ancients: Book Two of the Three Worlds Chronicles
- Act I: A Middle School Drama Anthology

## CONNECT WITH JAMES NORWOOD

- Twitter: https://twitter.com/jrnorwood
- Facebook: https://www.
  facebook.com/authorjnorwood
- Instagram: https://www.
  instagram.com/jrnteach/
- On the Web: https://www.
  threeworlds.net
- Subscribe to Newsletter: https://
  drjrn.com/newsletter

# PROLOGUE

In the deep and frozen blackness of space they waited. The passage of centuries did not cool their fury. They set their sights on a trio of worlds. One they would enslave, one they would destroy, and one they would teach. A thousand years in the past they were banished from their home and doomed to roam the stars in ancient ships not capable of sustaining them. Traveling between the stars took a generation, and when they finally found a home, it was barely habitable – rocky and dry and barren. They settled, and they grew, and they evolved until finally they had made the planet in their image, and yet a thousand years is not long enough to overcome the fury that the complete destruction of an entire society creates. As they grew and transformed, their hatred and wrath increased. Their anger overflowed until finally, in a fit of immense rage, they blasted into the stars destroying anything that stood in their way.

They would find their way home and on their journey they would instill fear into lesser civilizations. They would no longer be the dispossessed. They would become the conquerors. They set their sights on their former home, but they no longer belonged there. They would rain destruction down upon their hated forebears. Then they would reach out and take as their own a small blue world barely in its infancy. A world of water and light yet ravaged by war and famine. They would repossess another which they had lost.

Nothing could stop them. To the Negotiator and her legion, the time was right to strike. They would cool their fires on those lesser beings and in so doing prove to their ancestors irrevocably that they were the true Masters of the galaxy. Theirs was the true path, and only in despair would the worlds be cleansed.

They were coming, and soon every being on every world in every corner of the galaxy would know their name. Their name would be whispered in prayers and shouted in fear. The dead would tremble, and the living would faint at the name D'lai.

# PART 1

## PART I - IT BEGINS

# CHAPTER 1

"Space is really big." Gallagher thought to himself at the moment he found himself floating about with only an environmental suit, a severed life-support tether, and his confused thoughts to keep him company.

Seconds earlier, Gallagher had been trying to repair damage to an external solar panel while humming the tune to some annoying advertisement he had been unlucky enough to see one too many times on his pad. He stretched an arm out, straining to reach a sheared off bolt after a rather precarious journey through an asteroid field. Those micro-meteorites did significant damage to the more delicate exterior portions of the ship. That was when all hell broke loose. All hell, at least, for Major Cormac Gallagher. One instant he was going about his task, and in the next, he was bobbing along, untethered and all alone in empty space.

"Damn," said Gallagher.

Less than a minute earlier onboard *The Avenger*, Navigator Arvesp Erth shouted "Uh... Captain!" while staring in disbelief at her console. Annoyed at being interrupted from his own task, the Captain, a strong and rather sizable specimen of his species, twisted in his too small command chair toward the voice of the Navigator. He had been dozing off a little as he sat there. The recent mission they were on had been less than exciting, and Ziqna was just bored.

Glad for the distraction, he looked at the navigator. "What?" Captain Ziqna asked in his usual gruff voice. "What..." he started to repeat as an alarm on his console began beeping. "Navigator, why are we..." Klaxons began sounding from the cramped bridge, interrupting the Captain as the star field in a nearby window changed from a static array of stars to a jumble of blurred colors. "Emergency! All engines stop!" he said as everyone on the bridge began frantically scanning information on their own pads and workstation consoles.

"I have no control over the navigation computer," said Arvesp. "Most sensors are offline, controls not responding." Her fingers moved from one panel to another, attempting to regain control.

"Captain, we had personnel outside the ship when..." Security Officer Zika Uku stated more matter-of-factly than would be expected in such a crisis.

"That is not the worst part," mumbled Arvesp to herself as she turned to face the Captain. "The indicators says we haven't moved at all," she announced to the room, "yet, according to my readings, we are inside a gravity well!" *The Avenger* had been traveling in empty space preparing to engage the FTL drive.

"What? How is that...shut off those damn alarms" roared Ziqna, holding his hands over his ears to block out the blaring noise and the loud voices of his crew. "Everyone calm down. Let's assess what happened."

Security Officer Uku moved to his station while the bridge crew attempted to figure out what went wrong. Loud sounds emanated from somewhere deep below decks as the view outside went black, muting the stars. Everyone gasped as the lights and gravity blinked out as well. Silent black weightlessness engulfed Arvesp as her zero-g training kicked in.

The deck of the bridge was swallowed in darkness. "No, not entirely dark," she thought as she drifted in a controlled movement toward the emergency grip on the nearest bulkhead. Grabbing on, she almost spun out of control at her excitement as she gripped the handle a little too hard. Her body hit the wall as she tried to identify the origin of light. Everyone stopped talking when the illumination went out, but now a small stirring of voices could be heard from the other side of the cabin. Arvesp allowed her body to rotate as she searched for the source of the dim glow.

"There!" A small indicator light flashed from her station. Dread seeped in as Arvesp realized with sudden rapidity what exactly the light meant. Even with a near total loss of power, the emergency backup systems always provided power to this particular warning -- an intruder.

Major Cormac Angus Gallagher floated in space for what felt like hours, when in reality only minutes passed. After a moment, the surrounding stars went from blurred lines to pinpricks in the darkness. He scanned the area around him for any sign of *The Avenger*. Nothing. He checked his arm controller for any information it relayed. Too low for comfort, his oxygen level slowly dropped. He had been about to finish his spacewalk when things got weird. His communications unit showed no vessel or person in range, and yet his sensors detected an enormous source of gravity nearby.

"That's odd," Gallagher said to himself, "a gravity well...from what?" He detected no nearby planets or asteroids behind his sun visor. At least three standard units distant, the star in this system shone dimly, so that wasn't the source.

"Could it?" Gallagher had been trained in various scenarios for being in danger outside his ship, so he began a routine, visual grid search of nearby space, using the markings on the inside of his visor to help him. He was midway through searching the area of space 90 degrees to his right when he noticed a shimmering in space. "Oh boy," Gallagher thought. "Not good...a cloaked ship."

The presence of a hidden craft might explain his sudden untethered spacewalk. It wouldn't explain the location of *The Avenger*, though. He had a more pressing problem. Who in this region of space possessed cloaked ships? Gallagher prayed he was wrong.

On the darkened bridge, Arvesp's eyes adjusted to

the small amount of available light. She could now make out the forms of the other members of the crew. Ziqna kept trying in vain to seat himself back in his command chair. One or two other crew members, one human and one Gathung, like herself, held on to similar hand rails along the far side of the bridge. Startled, Arvesp caught the furtive movements of the nearby Security Officer, Zika Uku. Arvesp wasn't sure, but she thought she glimpsed him trying to open the door to the outer passageway.

"Why would he do that?" she thought to herself. "We have no idea what is out there." She launched herself from her hold toward the Security Officer. Zika was unaware of her presence as she grabbed a hand hold next to his substantial, almost elongated head.

The Gathung are a rather tall and inelegant species. Originating from the planet Gathung'l in a region of the Milky Way called The Orion Arm, most Gathung are from one of two major continents. As the most southern continent on Gathung'l, inhabitants of Sumor tended to be stockier and have darker skin than their northern neighbors on Naomor. Most inhabited worlds in the galaxy had only one dominant species of bipedal creatures, except for Gathung'l.

Two distinct groups of bipeds evolved. The planet's dominant species, the Gathung, are divided into two classes, The My, and the Ly. The My (all males), had elongated heads, long, almost reed-thin arms, and are covered in various shades of fur. The Ly (all females), had a similar build as The My, but are completely bare of all hair or fur. To decorate their bodies, most My wrapped themselves in colorful dresses, called My'un. Almost every member of the crew of *The Avenger* were Gathung as most other sentient races could not stand their stench. Humans, having a much weaker sense of smell than the Gathung, didn't seem to be bothered by the aroma, and so would willingly serve with the much more odorous species.

"Zika...what are you doing?" whispered the Navigator. Startled, Zika turned toward her. Arvesp observed with shock the blastgun unholstered and in his hand. Without thinking, she released her hand-hold and pushed off the wall with her strong legs. Too late. A brilliant bolt of amber light shot out of the blastgun. The bolt missed Arvesp's neck and whizzed off, hitting the opposite wall in a shower of sparks and melting electronics. Everyone on the bridge turned their heads toward the sound of the blaster bolt hitting the wall, missing the scuffle between the navigator and the security officer. Without warning, gravity and lights returned to the deck and everyone landed, most of them unharmed, on the floor of the bridge.

Arvesp remembered the intruder alert lighting up her panel at the same instant that another amber bolt shot from Zika Uku's blastgun, hitting her in the left leg. Too weak, the bolt failed to penetrate her tough skin. Nevertheless, the searing nerve pain caused Arvesp to cry out. Noticing his failure, Zika stood, pressed a small button next to the still closed exit and rushed through the open door leading off the bridge, running down the corridor while randomly shooting his blastgun behind him as he fled.

One or two beings jumped out of his way as he ran, a few uttering angry shouts in his direction. Arvesp, limping but still functional, raced down the corridor after Zika. She was unarmed, and so she avoided the bolts flung in her direction by his careless firing. He came upon a larger human who entered the corridor and slammed headlong into the taller man. The human, a civilian engineer named Corey Hodges, grabbed the security officer and wrestled the depleted blastgun from his grip.

CORMAC GALLAGHER WAS BORN AND RAISED NEAR Los Angeles, on Earth. Born a little over eighteen years before the Cathari made their first appearance in the sky, he was among the first generation of humans to answer the age-old question that plagued so many generations before, "are we alone?"

Gallagher spent his early years with his parents in a small house in Riverside, California. The previous decade had been tumultuous for the planet as a whole but this particular area of the country had been ravaged by economic disasters that left the area impoverished and full of violence. The middle of the twenty-first century had seen escalating conflict after conflict. Now it seemed as if the whole world was either on fire, bone dry, or starving. Then, the real fun began. The Cathari made their first appearance shaking most of the planet to its core. Gallagher's family decided it was way past-time to leave the area and moved farther north, as far away from packed population centers as possible.

Gallagher and his family spent the next several years moving from one small town to another. It took Gallagher's father more than a year to find a job he felt was suitable. Even the nagging of Gallagher's mother and the sad accommodations they found didn't spur him on as fast as the family hoped. Eventually, they settled in the extreme north of California. Gallagher's father, a lawyer by trade, set up shop in a tiny store front and finally decided that they were home. Gallagher and his two younger sisters enrolled in the local schools, and everyone tried to forget about aliens.

After Gallagher graduated from High School, life presented him with two opposing opportunities. He could serve in the US Army, or go to prison. He fell in with a bad sort during his last year of school and stole an air transport as part of a senior year prank. Naturally, he got caught. His parents were devastated by his behavior and local law enforcement wasn't too happy about it either. His lawyer negotiated and got the charges reduced but only if he would agree to serve at least four years in the military. Gallagher felt sure he did not want to join at a time of war, but he surely didn't want to spend those same four years locked in a cell. He agreed.

Joining the military changed his life. He learned discipline, honor, and self-respect. A natural athlete and brilliant in mathematics and linguistics, he rose through the ranks and at the end of his mandatory four year stint, he opted to re-enlist. Toward the end of his second enlistment, the Cathari re-emerged after having been gone for ten years. The first appearance by the Cathari had resulted in planet wide chaos. The second appearance of the Cathari was just after the planet wrapped up a successful attempt at unifying. Humans were not fooled by the reappearance. It was generally believed that the strides the planet had made toward peace was the motivating factor in their re-emergence. Most of the soldiers Gallagher knew and worked with showed deep apprehension of the visitation but Gallagher happened to be intrigued by them.

"If ya'll think those aliens are here to make friends, you must get your head examined," said a bunk mate of Gallagher to his buddies one evening. "They only came to enslave us."

"I don't think an advanced alien race would travel all that distance only to come and steal our skin or whatever it is you think they want," said Gallagher.

"I don't know about any of that, but I've seen enough on TV to make me think."

"TV?" Gallagher laughed. "How would TV have any idea what is *really* out there?"

The two men argued back and forth for a bit. Gallagher finally shook his head and got up to leave.

"We have a review in the morning gents. We should hit the bunks."

When the Cathari offered to train humans on Cathar Prime as part of their attempt to introduce the planet to the wider galactic community, Gallagher jumped at the opportunity and within six months he found himself studying off world.

His superiors in the Army recognized his aptitude and willingness to engage with the Cathari and before they agreed to ship him off planet, they gave him orders that made him none too happy. The US Army, now a branch of the United Nations Peacekeeping Force, ordered Gallagher to report back on everything he witnessed and experienced on Cathar Prime. Of most primary interest to his superiors was the military readiness of the Cathari. Military leaders on Earth suspected there was more behind the Cathari Alliance than they were led to believe, and they did not want to be unprepared. Humanity didn't understand the so-called peaceful ideals of the aliens and suspected far more sinister motives behind all this friendly exploration.

Gallagher didn't believe there were any bad intentions on the part of the Cathari, but he agreed to report back. The morning he was due to leave Earth, he gathered as much as he was allowed to bring with him and made his last calls to his family. Even though he did not expect anything to happen, this was space travel after all, and he was a little nervous.

He reported to the launch site and was amazed at the size and scope of the Cathari lander. It was twice the size of any space going vessel Gallagher had ever seen. It was most definitely larger than anything Earth had ever launched. Even the ships that carried colonists to Mars weren't nearly this big. Gallagher expected to be strapped down and in a space suit. When he entered the craft, he was led to a spacious seating area and given a short briefing on the trip.

It would take them less than three days at faster than light speed to travel from Earth to Cathar Prime. Gallagher was assigned temporary guest quarters and ate lunch with a dozen other volunteers. The ship blasted into orbit so smoothly that no one among the humans even realized they were en route until a voice came over a loudspeaker to inform them that there would be an almost imperceptible shift from natural gravity to artificial gravity.

The first time Gallagher saw deep space he was overwhelmed by not only the enduring beauty but also the absolute abyss of it all. The ship traveled to its

FTL injection coordinates and as it did so, Earth vanished and all he could see were innumerable stars. As the ship made its way to Cathar Prime, Gallagher and the other humans learned about interacting with their new hosts, gained some history of the planet, and were drilled in manners and action that would either please or sorely offend the Cathari people.

On Cathar Prime, he experienced wonders few other humans have ever seen or imagined. He met dozens of representatives from other species, learned about space exploration, extra-planetary naval tactics, star ship engineering, and he experienced first hand the vastness of the galaxy. The next two years while he studied at the Imperial Academy was going to be amazing.

As he had been ordered to, he dutifully reported back all his observations and his superiors rewarded him with ever-increasing rank and subsequent access to secret intelligence. Gallagher learned of his planetary leaders working with another alien species that held similar militaristic views as Earth did. As part of their collaboration with the Gathung, Earth began developing the technology to cloak an entire planet. Earth already independently developed the ability to cloak its space going vessels, but this goal superseded everything else. If successful, Earth and any other planet with the technology could literally hide from the outside universe.

Now a Major, Gallagher graduated from the Imperial Academy, and he received orders to report to his new station onboard *The Avenger*. His public role was determined to be Second Engineer. He would retain his rank of Major but this placement was a civilian placement so his rank would play no role other than as a formality. His superiors on Earth instructed him that his real job was to keep an eye on the development of the planet cloaking tech. Earth wanted to make sure that not even the Gathung, their supposed friends, would be able to steal the technology. They wanted it first, and they wanted to be the only planet that employed it.

First Engineer Hodges screwed up his face in puzzlement. Seconds ago while sipping his hot coffee, he mentally prepared himself for the day ahead. Each day he began by reviewing any action items his team of engineers compiled from the previous day's work. A ship like *The Avenger* needed constant upkeep and maintenance to keep in tip-top shape. He assigned his engineers to specific job functions and at the end of each day, they would record a log of everything that had either been completed, or was still in progress. The frequent trips between Earth and Gathung'l taxed the ships systems.

Hodges checked off this list of action items as the star field outside shifted and then went black. Setting down his coffee, he stood from his work station when he saw the system status monitor change from green to yellow.

"What in the world..." he began as he skimmed through the information displayed. According to his reports, several deck plates showed a "needs repair" status indicator. Chief Engineer Hodges glanced around the Engine Room. He appeared to be alone. Ten minutes earlier, after a short meeting of all his staff, he sent them on their way to perform their daily functions. Grunting in mild annoyance, Hodges grabbed a pad, rose from his chair, and left the Engine Room.

Hodges checked the location of the damaged deck plating and headed in that direction. On the way, he recalled a rather terse conversation with his Second Engineer, Major Gallagher.

"I need you to repair some solar panels that have been damaged." Hodges said earlier that morning.

"You mean grunt work?" Gallagher said in response. "My assignment has been to get the new security reactors up and running."

Annoyed and not terribly interested in what Gallagher thought about work assignments, Hodges replied, "not grunt work. Today it is your work."

"Can't someone else do it? I don't like space walks," said Gallagher.

"Just do it Gallagher," Hodges said before returning to his review of the logs.

"Okay boss. Whatever you say," Gallagher responded sarcastically before heading off to the airlock prep room.

Arriving at the first damaged deck plate, Hodges bent down and examined it. He grew concerned because the deck plating had tight tolerances with the other plating and an observer shouldn't see any gaps without the proper instrumentation. This deck plate looked like it had been lifted and then placed back down haphazardly. Scanning the corridor, he detected a few other plates skewed.

Hodges experienced a sinking feeling, and he began to repair the deck plating when he heard shouts coming from the entrance to the bridge. To his shock, the Security Officer, the Navigator and the Captain chased each other down the corridor to where he currently crouched. Zika had his blastgun out and repeatedly fired it behind him, though not well as he missed anything important except some now scorched interior panels.

Hodges tripped Zika as he attempted to pass, then eyed the others. Zika fell to his knees, his blaster tumbling from his hands.

"Hey, what is all this about?" shouted Hodges as he grabbed a hold of Zika.

Arvesp, by now caught up with the security officer, replied "He shot me!"

Hodges glanced down at Zika as more crew from the bridge came into sight, accompanied by the Captain. "Why are you shooting? Arvesp isn't a threat to you!"

"She attacked me first!" yelled Zika. "I merely defended myself!" Everyone paused for a moment, then several voices started shouting and exclaiming at the same time.

"He had his blastgun drawn when the gravity and power went out!" said a visibly angry Arvesp.

Growing in anger himself and having had enough

of the nonsense, the Captain roared "Enough!" Startled, everyone in the corridor fell silent and turned in his direction. The Gathung among the group kept their eyes down in submission. Hodges looked on with a look of curiosity on his face. Ziqna motioned to two nearby security personnel. "Put them in holding," he said, pointing a finger at Zika and then at Arvesp, "and secure that blastgun!" Arvesp started to protest but a fiery look from the Captain silenced her. Turning angrily toward Hodges, he asked, "Engineer, why are you in this corridor? Your station is three decks down"

Hodges calmly reflected for a moment before responding. "Captain, I was repairing some misaligned deck plating when all of you ran down the corridor"

Hearing Hodges continue speaking while being shoved away into a lift, Arvesp muttered something unintelligible. No one heard the rest of her protest.

Shaking his head, the Captain peered down the hall. "Everyone back to work." He motioned in the general direction of the holding cells. "Follow me Hodges." Ziqna strolled in the opposite direction as the rest of the bridge crew. Hodges picked up his tools and followed.

Captain Ziqna ran headlong into several members of the crew as he huffed down the hall toward the holding cells. Even though the majority of the crew onboard *The Avenger* was Gathung, a smattering of humans and other species served on board. As part of the mission of the Cathari Alliance, diversity among the various crafts of the fleet ranked among the top priorities when choosing who or what to fill each of the many roles with. *The Avenger* was no exception.

What the Captain and his superiors did not realize was that among the various races of the crew, three members, two Gathung and one human, were strategically placed in the ranks. These crew members did not work toward fulfilling the Cathari Alliance's objectives. In fact, the mission of *The Avenger* itself did not align with the long term plans of the Alliance. Earth and Gathung'l were working together on a top secret security project that they would prefer their Cathari colleagues to not know about. Zika Uku was a spy, placed onboard by the D'lai Authority. He had been ordered to watch and report back to D'lai leadership on events onboard *The Avenger*. As part of his association with the D'lai, he understood what the power loss earlier meant, being privy to some top secret intelligence on how the D'lai interact with other civilizations. Zika had one fatal flaw, however. He was a bit of a coward. A coward afraid of being caught.

Zika Uku also happened to be a criminal -- at least in the eyes of the D'lai. The D'lai took criminality to extreme heights. If a being had parents, grandparents, cousins, etc. who offended the D'lai, every member of that family would be branded a criminal. Zika's grandfather fought in the resistance and been executed by the D'lai. They used this to recruit Zika and press him into service. In fact, while the D'lai left Gathung'l, they still very much operated on the planet. Many Gathung became trapped by this and served The D'lai Authority.

"Sit!" barked Ziqna as he entered the small and sparsely furnished holding area. He motioned to two good sized chairs near a porthole. Arvesp glanced at Hodges, who then stared at Zika. When no one took claim to the only two chairs in the room, the Captain grunted and pointed at Hodges. Taking the hint, Corey Hodges sad down and waited. The Captain took the only other remaining chair near a too small desk.

Looking at the Security Officer, the Captain said "Why are you firing your blastgun on board my ship?"

Zika fidgeted nervously, which made Hodges react by covering his nose and mouth with his hands. When a Gathung was nervous he emits an odor that is utterly unpleasant so the other Gathung in the room didn't react to the malodorous Security Officer. They stared at him, waiting for a reply.

"I thought there was an intruder on the bridge," lied Zika Uku hopefully. "I was protecting..."

"An intruder?" interrupted the Captain skeptically. "An intruder from where? How would they have gotten on the bridge with no power to the doors?"

"He's lying" said the Navigator. "He tried to get off the bridge."

Chief Engineer Hodges shifted in his chair. The only human in the room, he grew more uneasy. If a Gathung stank when nervous, the room became even more stinky with three of them.

Earlier, Ziqna read recent reports from Earth and Gathung commands of odd behavior of star ships in other sectors of the galaxy. He was well aware that something was going on. What exactly that was, he only guessed at. The behavior of his Security Officer set his mind roiling with the possibilities.

"Leave the bridge...to go where?" said the Captain. "Wouldn't the bridge be the precise place for a Security Officer during an emergency?"

Zika again appeared uncomfortable and ignored the groans of Hodges. "Yes...sir," said the Security Officer. "I panicked."

"Panicked!" said the Captain. "Enough. I don't have time for a panicked security officer. You will be confined here until I have time to sort this whole *vdawt* out." He pressed a button on a console, stood and walked to the door. "Hodges we need to talk. Arvesp, go to your quarters."

The Navigator swiftly left the room. Ziqna gaped at his Security Officer with a look of distaste, then motioning to Hodges to follow, strolling out of the room as two junior security officers entered. "Lock him in a cell." He stomped down the hall, shaking his head. A passing Scree crew member squeaked and flattened itself against the bulkhead. Ziqna didn't even notice.

STILL FLOATING OUTSIDE, GALLAGHER WAS examining the shimmering outline of the alien ship. He recognized from experience that only a few sentient races had crafts capable of cloaking. His own planet perfected the technique only recently, but it was improbable that a human star ship would be this far out into The Orion Arm. Humans tended to be mildly xenophobic and only the most adventurous of humans ventured beyond their own solar system. Gallagher, being one of them, left Earth the moment he was legally allowed to and headed off into deep space aboard a Cathari frigate.

He had been among the first humans to have been accepted into the Imperial War College on Cathar Prime, one of the nearest inhabited systems to Earth. The Cathari were members of an interplanetary alliance spanning two dozen inhabited systems. Earth had been invited to join the alliance upon achieving a single world government, but the leaders of the planet, in an extraordinarily close vote, declined the invitation. The Cathari, unconvinced by humanity's xenophobia, established an embassy in London, the new capital of a united Earth. Over the next few years, other planets, including the Gathung, would send embassies as well, allowing Earth to maintain loose contact with the galaxy at large.

Gallagher wore on his tool belt an emergency tether, and he now decided it was time to attempt to reel himself into the unknown vessel. He took aim at an area he thought might be near an external hatch, and fired. The magnetic head of the tether latched on to the cloaked vessel, and after depressing a button on his controls, he was whisked toward the surface. He slammed into the hull and if not for the tether he would have tumbled backward into space.

"Now what" thought Gallagher. He found the hull, but how would he get inside? The answer was not long in coming, as a light flared from nearby. It was disconcerting to see light emanating from nothing, but Gallagher was moderately relieved that someone inside detected his presence. A being covered head to toe in an environmental suit similar in size and shape to his own emerged from the light. Gallagher didn't recognize the markings on the suit as the being moved in the zero gravity of space toward his location. The alien grabbed the head of the tether with one arm, depressed the release mechanism of the strong magnet, and attached the tether to himself.

The unknown space walker then moved back toward the light source and pulled Gallagher inside.

After a few moments, the airlock pressurized and Gallagher watched the unknown rescuer remove its helmet. Gallagher stepped back in surprise to find the alien seemed very much like a human with one frightening exception. The alien's skin was a mottled gray and absolutely no hair at all on his bulbous head.

"Whoa..." Gallagher said in surprise. "What's up with your skin buddy?"

The alien peered quizzically at Gallagher and said, "I could ask you the same thing, buddy."

Gallagher was surprised that the alien spoke Standard as well as he did. Having met dozens of races in his time outside the Sol system, he almost always used a translator device attached behind his left ear to understand other beings. This guy spoke his own language.

The alien seemed to sneer at Gallagher over before replying further. "Remove your helmet, human."

Gallagher hesitated, then he shrugged and pulled his own space helmet off. He figured that if this alien wanted to harm him, all he needed to do was release the tether and let Gallagher continue floating in empty space. Gallagher breathed the air a little hesitantly, sniffed a little at the odd odor, then looked around him at the cramped but efficient airlock chamber.

"So, what's up with this ship? Why is it cloaked?" Gallagher asked.

The alien smiled and responded. "We didn't want the others to see us."

Gallagher attempted to get more out of the alien, but he motioned for Gallagher to follow him out of the airlock and down a short corridor. Gallagher did as he was instructed and followed behind the strange alien. The two of them entered a small, windowless room that contained nothing more than two chairs and a small desk. The alien took up a seat behind the desk and pointed at the only remaining seat.

"Sit down, please," the alien said.

Gallagher was surprised by the pleasant tone in the alien's voice. If he had been in this other guy's shoes, he didn't know if he would be quite as pleasant. As he sat down, he examined the grey-skinned alien more closely. He detected significant differences between this alien's appearance and the typical human's skin-color. The alien had much larger than average eyes, a huge almost rounded head, and where a nose should be, Gallagher only saw small holes. He rubbed his eyes, remembering stories from childhood and a shiver ran down his spine. The alien busied himself with a small pad on the desk, an eyebrow arching in an unnervingly human-like gesture before proceeding.

"What were you doing outside your ship, human?"

"Gallagher."

"Hmm?" asked the alien, puzzled.

"My name. It's Gallagher."

Staring at Gallagher, he continued. "I asked what you were doing outside your ship, not what your name is... Gallagher."

Gallagher returned the stare. "Most humans don't like being referred to as 'human'. We kinda like our own names."

The alien nodded in a gesture decidedly unlike a typical human nod and waited for a response to his query.

Gallagher sighed then responded, "I was repairing a solar panel."

Seeing Gallagher was not going to volunteer any more information, he continued with his questioning. "And what made you deploy a tether?"

Gallagher snorted before responding. "Well, if I hadn't, I'd still be floating out there wouldn't I?"

Unperturbed by Gallagher's sarcastic tone, he continued. "Yes. Why did you deploy your tether into open space?" he persisted.

"It wasn't open space. I could tell there was something cloaked."

The alien nodded, again in that inhuman fashion.

"Listen, if you're gonna ask me nonsense questions, I'd rather be left alone," Gallagher said. "Maybe let me go back to my own ship."

"What is your position aboard *The Avenger*?"

This last question seriously concerned Gallagher. "Um. Hmm," was all he got out as his mind whirled. While he was technically an engineer, he was assigned other more secretive duties he really didn't want this alien, or any alien in fact, to know.

The alien looked up and waited for a response.

Gallagher frowned but responded as he didn't want to upset his unfamiliar host, "Second Engineer.".

"Why send a second engineer out to repair a solar panel?" asked the alien.

"I don't know...maybe ask the First Engineer," Gallagher said.

Frustrated at the responses, the alien sighed

before continuing. "Fine." He pushed a button on his pad and the chair Gallagher was sitting in speedily and without warning cuffed both of his arms and both of his legs. "Hey that's a little tight!" protested Gallagher before the alien responded further. All at once the alien stood and strolled from the room without a word.

"Damn," Gallagher said for the second time in less than an hour.

THE D'LAI WAS PERHAPS THE MOST MYSTERIOUS species in the known galaxy. No living sentient had ever knowingly seen an individual D'lai. The D'lai always appeared in flowing robes that hid everything, including their faces. Among the various planets, however, no one feared the D'lai more than the Gathung. Approaching two hundred years prior, when the Gathung first began venturing into orbit around their planet and explored their home system, the D'lai swept in and seized control of the Gathung'l system.

Thousands of ordinary Gathung died in the purge that followed. Any individual found to not be in top genetic form had been killed or sterilized and put into work camps. Others who opposed the brutal rule of the D'lai were blinded, mutilated, and often executed -- all publicly. Needless to say, any public resistance died down fast and the Gathung began a century of enslavement to the D'lai Authority.

After almost one hundred years of rule, the D'lai vanished from the system overnight. Unconstrained and without the harsh rule of the D'lai, the Gathung broke out into clan wars which threatened to destroy the vestiges of society that remained. After two years of almost constant fighting, a Ly called Kwiu Zig rose to power on the Naomor continent and rapidly consolidated his authority and military strength. His clan warriors overnight seized control of the southern-most continent of Sumor as well.

The enslavement by the D'lai Authority reeked havoc on Gathung culture, but it was not without its benefits. One such benefit was a planet-wide infrastructure of rail systems, ground and air travel the occupiers built out of necessity. Using this transportation network, Kwiu Zig had been able to overtake even the most remote regions of the planet. He easily installed himself as First Dictator, a job he made up, and he harshly consolidated the remaining Gathung people under one rule of law.

Another advantage of the D'lai occupation had been the technology to travel between the stars. A century earlier, the Gathung had barely perfected chemical propulsion systems when they fell under D'lai rule. Now, thanks to the slavery of the planet, the Gathung understood the workings of the FTL drives that bent space and propeled a spacecraft faster than light. Gathung engineers had been trained by the D'lai to repair their damaged ships, providing critical knowledge to the Gathung.

What puzzled the Gathung more than anything was the unanticipated and sudden disappearance of the D'lai. If not for the wisdom of Kwiu Zig, many of the ordinary Gathung would probably not have understood the value and importance of the discarded D'lai technology. First Dictator Zig promptly seized on what that technology meant and set about to prepare his planet in case the D'lai came back.

A long-lived species, the united Gathung began colonizing other planets in their system before venturing out into deep space. Dozens of light years from Gathung, the Cathari had already begun establishing its loose alliance of worlds. The Gathung, led by the First Dictator, joined The Cathari Alliance only seventeen years after the D'lai vanished. A species that never looked backwards, the Gathung plunged headlong into interplanetary politics and expeditiously emerged as an able if boring species.

Natural bureaucrats, the Gathung insinuated themselves in every level of The Cathari Alliance and soon assumed a major voice in any decision made by The Alliance. As a result, they spread among the stars without realizing their former captors, the D'lai, still spied on them and waited.

The Gathung also began a campaign to find other worlds, aligned or not, that shared a similar goal of not just interplanetary cooperation, but planetary defense. Several years after the Cathari established its embassy on Earth, the Gathung began making secret overtures with the humans about their hopes and ideas for planetary defense. They had no intention of allowing the D'lai or any other unknown conquering species to create chaos for them again. The humans, for their part, eagerly got to work.

On board the D'lai ship *The Spector*, Negotiator Ret D'iash remotely watched the interactions between Major Gallagher and a security officer who brought him onboard. D'iash was furious at the security officer having revealed himself. She would deal with the officer later. However, since he was not D'lai, she had no fear of revealing her people's deepest secret. D'iash had rarely encountered a human before, so she was puzzled by the attitude of the man toward the being who rescued him from the vacuum of space. D'iash sat back in her chair after the interrogation ended and tapped the edge of his desk in contemplation. D'iash had been monitoring the Cathari Alliance when her crew stumbled across *The Avenger*. The Gathung were not in the normal space lanes and so the Negotiator had decided to capture and inspect the much smaller Gathung vessel. Negotiator D'iash was curious as to why the normally predictable Gathung would be so far from normal routes, and she was determined to get to the bottom of it.

Already, she dispatched reconnaissance officers onto *The Avenger* after the capture. It was standard operating procedure for the D'lai to disable any captured ship by disrupting gravity, lights, and most power sources. The dispatched recon team wore magnetic boots which enabled them to walk in an almost normal fashion despite the loss of gravity. Each recon team member also wore a small shield which rendered them invisible in normal light. Their mission was to gather information from the Gathung data banks and get off before the D'lai would ordinarily restore systems and release them -- mostly unharmed. With any luck, the recon team's presence would go undetected. The D'lai were preparing for war and Negotiator D'iash wanted any inside information on the Cathari Alliance she could gather prior to her arrival in the Cathari system.

All D'lai ships traveled using their cloaking technology. The technology enabled them to monitor galactic events without being directly or indirectly involved. The only time the D'lai involved themselves in planetary or galactic events was during their various conquests of newly discovered civilizations. The D'lai enjoyed keeping themselves mysterious as it made other planetary civilizations overly cautious and easy to manipulate.

"Negotiator?" a voice said from a pad near the D'iash. "We have retrieved copies of the data banks and our recon teams are back onboard."

"Good. Undock *The Avenger* and prepare to get underway," said the Negotiator.

"Yes Negotiator," said the voice.

A small rumbling vibration in the floor accompanied the undocking maneuver with the Gathung craft from the sizable hold. D'iash carefully considered what she would do with the human Gallagher and decided she would keep the human as a valuable source of additional information.

"The human may require more intense interrogation," D'iash mused aloud as the warship hurriedly departed on course to Cathar Prime. "He actually thinks he has seen one of us...what a fool," she laughed.

# CHAPTER 2

Cathar Prime is the only habitable planet in its system. Four other planets orbit the Cathari star. However, three distant gas giants and the only other rocky world all orbited outside the red dwarf's habitable zone. The Cathari system is one in a dense cluster of stars where life evolved. Innately curious, the Cathari grew aware early in their civilization that life existed elsewhere in the universe. They developed the means to learn about and interact with their stellar neighbors, and they were among the first in their region of the galaxy to develop interstellar travel. At first, traveling between stars at sub-light speeds was slow and time-consuming. Cathari scientists discovered new propulsion methods that made the trips between stars faster and more efficient. What once took decades, thanks to the development of the gravity FTL drive, now took days.

The Cathari were by nature a peaceful civilization. Many centuries passed since any real conflict took place on their planet. The result of that devastating war shaped future generations of Cathari. However, the memory of that time faded and over time only a few knew the dark secrets and shame that came from their own actions. Civilian and religious leaders began to teach of pacifism and tranquility. They took their love of peace and unnatural abhorrence of violence with them in their explorations of deep space. The Cathari had no interest in the planets of their own small star system, and so they developed more efficient methods of interstellar travel, and they found other space-faring worlds that shared their belief in peace, and formed what became known as The Cathari Alliance. Since the Cathari and its chosen allies spurned any form of militarism and aggression, they developed relatively weak planetary and ship-based defensive weapons systems to protect themselves. They instituted protocols for contact with other, less developed worlds. To be considered for contact by the Cathari or its allies, a planet had to have developed the ability to leave their own star systems. Their first interactions with Earth, several light years from their own system, taught them not all planetary civilizations were peaceful or wished to join them and that possessing the ability to travel in space did not mean a planet happened to be ready for interstellar diplomacy.

Earth began exploring other star systems but its planet was fractured by near-constant wars. The Cathari saw humanity as too violent, and they withdrew from contact. Earth, having answered the question "are we alone" moved to unify its planetary government and worked harder on its propulsion and space technologies, and most important to Earth, its planetary defenses.

The contact with Earth instilled in The Cathari Alliance further protocols that they would only make contact with planets that achieved peaceful, planetary governance. They feared what would happen if a violent species discovered them before they were ready.

The Gathung, a civilization just out of interstellar infancy when it joined The Cathari Alliance, provided the peace-loving Cathari with the opportunity to retire back to their home system after a chance encounter with the secretive D'lai left an entire fleet of Cathari ships floating dead in space. The bureaucratic Gathung enabled the work of maintaining the diverse and growing alliance to be managed by more willing hands, without endangering any more Cathari lives.

The D'lai, in contrast to the Cathari, dreamed of galactic conquest and despised the peaceful Cathari. Where the Cathari valued tranquility, the D'lai celebrated conquest. Where the Cathari valued openness and transparency, the D'lai believed they possessed the divine right to mask themselves in mystery and hide their motives.

The D'lai had been aware of The Cathari and learned of its alliance when it encountered the Cathari in a system they were attempting to conquer. The Cathari people as a whole were ignorant of the aggressive nature of the D'lai. Leaders on Cathar Prime possessed secret intelligence on the D'lai and worked to avoid contact with them whenever possible. The fleet commanders were not privy to the closely held secrets, and so they attempted to broker peace when the D'lai commander turned his weapons upon the Cathari. The resulting bloodbath taught the rank and file Cathari a valuable lesson and forced their attention inward. Unknown to the Cathari, the D'lai plotted for centuries its revenge on Cathar Prime. The D'lai actively monitored their home world and made long-term plans to destroy the alliance and install themselves as the galactic masters.

Due to the development of cloaking technology, the D'lai were able to directly monitor alliance worlds and recruit willing and unwilling conspirators to their cause. Instead of directly attacking the Cathari, the D'lai chose instead to undermine their attempts at peace. The D'lai considered the diplomacy of the Cathari to be aggression. Their own ancient history with Cathar Prime biased the D'lai to anything the Cathari did. Now, after a century of planning and subtle action, the D'lai were ready to make their move against the Cathari. Already, multiple planets had been infiltrated by the technologically superior D'lai. Worlds such as Gathung'l, Earth, and no less than seven Cathari colonies had D'lai agents among their ranks.

Orbiting one of the Cathar System's gas giants, a cloaked fleet of D'lai warships patiently awaited the arrival of Negotiator D'iash.

ONBOARD *THE AVENGER*, CAPTAIN QIK ZIQNA rubbed his head in contemplation and a fair share of frustration as he sat in a small office off the bridge. He had been the captain of this ship for a few years now, and he never had to investigate one of his own crew members for attempting to kill or maim another crew member. Of course, he'd never found himself out in space with no power and artificial gravity either. The ship always ran with precision so these new developments were giving him a headache.

Corey Hodges, who the Captain came across after the mysterious fighting between his navigator and security officer, had been explaining why he left his post.

"I saw warnings about misaligned deck plates and tried to figure out why there were misaligned in the first place," Hodges explained. "It was almost as if someone lifted them up a tiny fraction somehow and then the plating fell back in place. Right afterwards we lost our gravity and lights."

The Captain studiously ignored a flashing light emanating from his pad while considering what Hodges relayed. "Magnetic boots?" He surmised.

"Magnetic boots," Confirmed Hodges. "Or, more precisely, gravity boots."

Crew members wore gravity boots when they were working outside the ship. The artificial gravity generated by modern space craft only worked if you were actually inside that space craft. Instead of relying simply on suit based thrusters and tethers, a good pair of gravity boots enabled someone to walk along the outer hull. Sometimes, when a crew member came back inside the ship, they would walk around with the boots on and that would cause problems for the engineers who then needed to re-align the decking.

"Did you have any engineers wearing magnetic boots? Was the plating near the airlocks?"

"No, Captain. The only engineer...damn. Gallagher. He was repairing external solar panels when this all happened."

Captain Ziqna knew the unofficial job duties for Major Gallagher, so it surprised him that Hodges would send him to repair solar panels.

"Why was Gallagher doing that? Didn't he have other duties?"

"Someone had to and everyone else had things to

do," replied Hodges. "Anyway, I almost forgot about him entirely!"

Hodges went to a console and tried to raise Gallagher on the comms. No answer. Concern bloomed on his face as he searched external cameras. No sign of the engineer there either. Where is he?

"Gallagher is missing. If he isn't the one using his gravity boots, then..."

Hodges worried over the possible loss of Gallagher. He relied on Gallagher's expertise as they worked to bring the planet cloaking tech prototype online. The Captain must have also been worried because he promptly checked his pad and set about searching through the screens that popped up. His expression froze when he found what he probed for. He bound out of his chair, toppling it over, and rushed from the room. Hodges stared after him, apprehension on his face, before following him down the corridor toward the bridge.

The Captain burst onto the small bridge and accidentally slammed into a security officer on duty. "We've had an intruder. They've searched our databanks. Find out what else they may have stolen," said the Captain. Turning to operations. "We also have a missing crewman. Engineer Gallagher. Find him!"

The stunned security officer, a rookie on his first assignment, stood there with a blank expression on his face.

"NOW" roared the Captain. The frightened officer ran off the bridge as every pair of eyes turned back to its screens and panels. Noticing Hodges still following him, he motioned in the direction of the departed security officer. "Hodges, help him out. Find out how the intruders got on board."

Hodges nodded and left. Captain Ziqna left the bridge a moment later and headed to Arvesp's quarters. Barging in unannounced, he directed his attention on her. "What happened back there?"

Arvesp hurriedly relayed her actions and suspicions. Captain Ziqna listened impatiently.

"Zika?" repeated the Captain. "He fired on you." It was a statement, not a question, so Arvesp waited for him to go on. "He tried to leave the bridge, not secure it?"

Arvesp nodded. "Yes. When I asked him what happened, he fired on me."

The Captain nodded once more before stepping toward the door. "Get back to your station," He ordered before heading down the corridor once more.

Arvesp didn't even have to time to affirm the order before he left.

Humans were a proud species, and they liked to let every other species they encountered know how they felt. Gallagher was no different. He was not only proud of being a human, but he was very proud that he was one of the few humans in interstellar space. That is why sitting in this small room, confined, and confused, made Gallagher feel small. Which ever species controlled this ship, they didn't care about him at all.

Gallagher was also very bored. Sitting in a nondescript room with nothing on the walls, no portholes or windows, and only a utilitarian desk for something to look at was dull. In fact, he nearly dozed off from the sheer boredom when he heard a noise behind him. His interrogator returned. He twisted his head to look and gasped. The being in the room with him was not the same that brought him inside the ship. This particular being was not wearing the environmental suit but was covered head to toe in flowing green fabric. No, not fabric. Flowing green *something*.

Ret D'iash, the D'lai Negotiator, entered the small interview room that Gallagher was currently being held in. After a moment, and once she realized that she had been seen, she walked around the chair Gallagher was confined in, her traditional green *sdawij* flowing around her. She settled in the chair behind the desk, her eyes never leaving Gallagher.

*"Riaẓ am Ret D'iash. Fl'ṣawv kia D'lai,"* The Negotiator said in way of greeting.

Gallagher looked at the alien, his eyes puzzled. He shook his head, confused.

"That other fellow spoke Standard," said Gallagher. "I don't know what you said buddy."

The Negotiator did not appear to hear or understand, repeating herself once more. After a moment, she activated a switch on the desk and seconds later another D'lai crewman entered the room.

*"Mëvai!"* said The Negotiator. *"Oi buit uilyi dü."*

Gallagher waited impatiently, looking from one alien to another. This new alien was not the same as captured him and was also wearing one of those head to toe not quite fabric outfits. Both these aliens were taller and seemed more elegant somehow. They reminded him of another species, but he couldn't put his finger on it. The new alien looked in the direction of Gallagher, and after The Negotiator repeated for a third time her introduction, the alien translated in somewhat passable Standard, saying, "This be Ret D'iash. She Negotiator of D'lai."

Of course Gallagher was unsure what a Negotiator was beyond the common meaning of the word. "Why am I here?" he began, "Here I was, minding my own business when you fellas came along."

The D'lai translator paused for perhaps too long a moment before repeating what Gallagher hoped was a good translation of what she said. The Negotiator replied in her native tongue so Gallagher waited, again, for a translation. The translator actually looked like he was nervous underneath all that not-fabric, shifting a little as he said "Negotiator says human is *dü*, stupid. Human should not leave *ë*. How say *ë* – place of home?" struggled the translator.

Gallagher thought for a moment. "Home...Earth...um planet..."

"Planet. Yes. Human should not leave own planet."

"This is going nowhere," Gallagher thought to himself. "Yes...but why am I here?"

The translator repeated in D'lai and after a few

breaths, the translator again spoke. "You will remain on ship. Negotiator has need of human."

That sounded ominous so Gallagher grunted. The Negotiator stood and swiftly left the room leaving Gallagher to wonder what this alien wanted with a human. "I hope it's to teach him better Standard," Gallagher said out loud as the room was once again empty.

"Damn."

NEGOTIATOR D'IASH LEFT THE INTERROGATION room, leaving Gallagher behind. She smiled to herself as she strolled down an exceptionally long corridor. D'lai design focused on function over form so it was normal for a D'lai ship to consist of long corridors with numerous offshoots leading to other sections. Despite this, D'iash wished the place was a little better organized. At three hundred standard years old, her people considered her to be elderly. This mission is critical to the long term plans of the D'lai and she held no intention of letting her age slow her down. Nevertheless, she felt tired when she finally made it to her small office.

Entering the compact, windowless room, D'iash sat behind a small but functional desk and began reading the screen. She received several messages from the D'lai Authority in the past few hours. Working rapidly, she prioritized them and began working her way through the list when her eyes were drawn to one flashing red: Important. She clicked open the message.

"First Dictator Zig arrived on Cathari Prime. Begin objective."

The Negotiator closed the message, logged out of the console and left the room for the bridge. After a short walk from her office to the bridge, a fact she felt grateful for, she entered the room and began issuing orders.

"Navigator, set course for Cathar Prime. Engage at maximum speed."

"Aye, Negotiator," concurred the Navigator. "Course laid in and engaged."

*The Spector* suddenly vanished from its present location, leaving *The Avenger* behind. Somewhere down in the bowels of the ship, Cormac Gallagher was still strapped into the restraint chair. In his isolated room, Cormac Gallagher understood what the mild vibrations in the decking meant. They were underway. He tried again to free himself from the restraints but without success.

"Damn these things are on tight!" Gallagher muttered. He wondered aloud if he was about to be a long-term guest. The thought of that made him struggle even harder. The more he struggled, however, the tighter the restraints seemed to get. Reluctantly, he gave up on freeing himself and instead focused his thoughts on his predicament. Gallagher didn't know who captured him or *The Avenger*, but he heard his fair share of rumors about capable species. Very few civilizations were believed to possess the ability to cloak. In fact, cloaking in any form was banned under Cathari Alliance treaties. The insanely peaceful Cathari believed hiding a spaceship was aggressive and fostered an atmosphere of mistrust among planets. That left only the non-aligned Earth who so far refused to play fair, at least according to the Cathari, and the galaxy's most mysterious species. The D'lai.

Gallagher learned of the D'lai occupation of Gathung'l when he was in the Imperial Academy. The wounds from that conquest were still fresh in the minds of the Gathung he soon became acquainted with. When he had been assigned to *The*

*Avenger,* he made it a point to learn as much as he could.

Even though no alien power ever conquered Earth, plenty of humans feared that possibility. Gallagher thought it would be a good idea for him to learn as much about it so that if, heaven forbid, Earth found itself in a similar situation, he might have some ideas on how to defend the planet.

Of course, he had no idea if the D'lai were even active and even if they were, would they really take another ship like someone took *The Avenger?* Gallagher shivered at the prospects of a civilization having that kind of power.

"Could this be a D'lai ship?" Gallagher thought to himself. "That's not good."

Kwiu Zig, the aging First Dictator of Gathung'l, gazed out a view window from his state-room aboard the Gathung flagship *Naomor.* Entering orbit of Cathar Prime, the *Naomor* brought the First Dictator and assorted Gathung nobles to Cathar Prime in celebration of the two hundredth anniversary of the alliance. They slipped into the crowded orbit occupied by dozens of others from many planets. Zig turned away from the window at the sound of his comm unit chiming.

"Yes?" asked the Dictator in mild annoyance.

"Excellency, we are in parking orbit. Cathari Ambassador Liuna sends her greetings," said the voice.

"Good. Prepare my shuttle."

The First Dictator unsteadily rose to his feet and left his quarters, accompanied by an aide. Late in his life, Kwiu Zig exhibited the usual signs of advanced age. He tried to keep his people from noticing his weakness, but as time went on, it became ever more difficult to mask his feebleness. He waved away any attempt at assistance provided by his aide, and walked down the corridor. He finally reached his small shuttle and settled gratefully into a seat as the small vessel left the hangar of *The Naomor* and made its way to the planet's surface.

Upon arrival of the First Dictator on the surface, the usual fanfare and overly flamboyant display of Cathari pride accompanied his arrival. Zig never enjoyed the smell of alien air. He much preferred the scented atmosphere of Gathung'l. He made it a point to visit as few planets as possible.

"Peace" greeted Ambassador Liuna to the arriving delegation. The Cathari were an elegant species, and always chose colorful outfits to accent their lithe, athletic bodies. The Ambassador was no exception and chose an ornate flowing dress of vibrant golds and blues, accenting her well-coiffed blonde hair. Zig briefly wondered why the Cathari didn't come up with a more original title for its planetary leader, but forthwith shook off the speculation. More important concerns weighed his thoughts down.

"Peace" replied the First Dictator in an automatic response, customary to members of The Alliance. He was about to rise from his seat when the world tilted sideways. The First Dictator slumped to his side, confused, as those around him ran up to him with concerned expressions. Recovering fast, he smiled weakly as he stood.

"Pardon an old man," the First Dictator laughed. "The change in gravity...disoriented me." Zig hoped his excuse would be enough to dissuade further considerations of his health. His aide, however, recognizing the symptoms of Zeisen Syndrome – a common ailment among the oldest Gathung – unobtrusively helped the ailing leader into a private room.

Zeisen Syndrome is a pernicious disease that affects roughly fifteen percent of Gathung over the age of two hundred. It worked to weaken the muscles and nervous systems of its victims until the unfortunate person is unable to control even the smallest muscle. Typically, Zeisen Syndrome worked slowly and often went unnoticed for years. However, in the case of First Dictator Zig, his heavy schedule and burdened life caused the symptoms to appear more rapidly. Those closest to the dictator suspected he had, at best, a year before he would be completely unable to move. Death would soon follow triggering planet-wide uncertainty as to who would next lead the Gathung civilization.

Ambassador Liuna strolled purposefully into the private room where First Dictator Zig was receiving an injection from his aide. She stopped in her tracks, concern blooming across her face.

"Kwiu..." she started to say when the First Dictator waved her over to a nearby couch.

"It's nothing, Liuna," responded Zig. "I'm just...old." He paused a moment before continuing. "My time is almost done."

Gathering her racing thoughts, the Ambassador replied, "And why did you come then? If you're ill, why not stay home? Others can manage in your place."

"I had to come. The Alliance is in danger." The Dictator motioned to his aide. "Bring me the data file."

The aide complied, handing the First Dictator a small pad. Kwiu Zig checked over the pad for a moment, then handed it to Ambassador Liuna. Her eyes went wide as she read the cramped text on the small screen.

"This... this is not possible," she stated. "The D'lai? Here?"

First Dictator Zig nodded. "We received intelligence that the D'lai have infiltrated every level of the Cathari Alliance and its member worlds. For all we know, they are already in this system doing who knows what."

The Ambassador tried unsuccessfully to hide the panic on her elegant Cathari face.

"We thought they'd left, given up."

Kwiu Zig shook his head. "No. We've expected for decades that we'd not seen the last of them. Why do you think I worked so hard to unify my people? It wasn't to avoid the mistakes of our past. It is to make us stronger. To give us...all of us... a chance." Zig kept to himself for now his secret alliance with Earth.

The First Dictator sensed another wave of vertigo overcome him. He pointed to his aide once more.

"We came because we need to prepare. Plans have been underway for some time to fight off the D'lai."

Ambassador Liuna, shocked, had no reply other than to say, "This alliance is *peaceful* Kwiu. Plans? Fight off? I need to consult my ministers. We need to figure out a..."

"No!" shouted the First Dictator. "You cannot bring this to them. For all we know, your council has been infiltrated! No. We must proceed – the two of us. Alone."

Ambassador Liuna dipped her head sadly as she pondered the implications and began to formulate a plan. "Earth is sending a representative for the celebrations and the Plenary Session. They are better suited than we are for *violence*." The Ambassador choked out. Her distaste was obvious. "We will need to approach him. Carefully." She had every intention on ignoring the emphatic demands of the First Dictator. She would consult her ministers. She needed to choose wisely which of them to speak to.

Zig thought over the planning that had been ongoing for several years now between his planet and Earth. He wondered if he should fill the Ambassador in on the planet cloaking plans but decided against it. She was too peaceful to understand and besides, how would he be absolutely sure she wasn't somehow working with the D'lai. Years of fighting left him cynical and supremely paranoid of the motives of others.

The two planetary leaders talked for a few more minutes before Ambassador Liuna excused herself. She needed time to think, to compose herself. She needed to come to terms with the fact that for all the peace initiatives of her people, none of those would stop the inevitable war that was to come.

"How will we deal with possibly millions of dead beings?" she mourned privately as she found solace in her small office. "What are we going to do?"

Out in the blackness of space, the ship carrying Negotiator D'iash arrived to join the cloaked D'lai fleet.

Decades ago, when the Cathari first made contact with Earth, the planet was still divided into individual countries – each vying for superiority. A large-scale conflict decimated The Middle East, and unscrupulous businessmen were busily scraping up anything that remained of the oil-rich region.

World leaders were holding a summit in Geneva, Switzerland, attempting to reconcile their nations and bring a level of stability to the planet when the Cathari entered orbit. Unlike rumors that persisted for many years of prior alien contact and secret government cover-ups, the Cathari boldly announced themselves to anyone who stared up into the sky.

Most humans feared a planetary conquest was about to begin, and so the unrest that followed the arrival of the Cathari puzzled the visitors. Their pronouncements of peace did little to stem the violence planet side, and so they withdrew, keeping an eye on the planet from a distance. However, the damage was done. Earth now realized it was not alone in the universe.

Seizing on the opportunity, the British Prime Minister persuaded other world leaders to stop fighting each other and start preparing for the alien menace. The planet easily united, granting more and more authority to the United Nations until that body was a true planetary government. Humanity set its sights upon the stars with greater effort than before. They organized colonial missions to Mars and the moons of Jupiter and Saturn. Earth scientists worked harder to develop better methods of propulsion, long distance communication, planetary defense, and space based weapon design.

Eventually, the Cathari made contact once more with a more unified Earth, establishing loose diplomacy with the planetary leadership. Earth, however, remained skeptical of the motives of their new "friends" and so refused to join their alliance. By this time, other sentient races made themselves known to humanity, including the Gathung. Many humans felt that Earth needed to remain independent if it stood any chance of developing as a galactic power. Others were more xenophobic and wanted little or no contact with alien races. The United Nations settled on a plan that would allow Earth to remain in contact with the Cathari while maintaining its neutrality. The Cathari agreed and with Earth's blessing, established an interplanetary embassy in London, the capital of a united Earth. Similar outposts was created on both Cathar Prime and Gathung'l.

Humanity was understandably skeptical of the motives of the Cathari, and the alliance as a whole. After all, the Cathari appeared and then vanished from Earth orbit at a time when the planet was still reeling from an era of war. It didn't make sense to the more violent humans that an alien species would travel presumably dozens of light years only to pop in, say hi, then leave. The Cathari, on the other hand, delighted in the minutiae of establishing a more permanent contact and earnestly hoped Earth would become a full member.

While Earth would accurately be described as having a single unitary government with a Planetary Secretary General, Legislative Assembly, and all the trappings that went along with that, it was not true to say that Earth was *completely* united. Each of the former countries still held their own cultural distinctions. Most of them even kept their own established governmental systems. The United States maintained its President, the British their Monarchy, etc. While these governments still existed based on national and regional pride and history, it was still a fact that Earth established a planetary government that regularly and systematically attempted to reign in these competing interests. It was *mostly* successful.

During those early days of planetary unity and contact with interstellar civilizations, the D'lai monitored events from deep space. They had not yet traveled to the Sol System but relied on their advanced technology to keep in touch with the various efforts by The Cathari Alliance and Earth to familiarize themselves with each other. The D'lai didn't expect that the fledgling Earth civilization would be any threat to its galactic objectives, but they also held no intention of ignoring Earth entirely. That was a strategic mistake on the part of the D'lai.

Earth, for its part, began to travel tentatively outside their own solar system. A century in the past they launched various probes like Voyager I and II, but those efforts took decades and humanity was, if nothing else, a little impatient. Even before the Cathari entered Earth orbit, NASA and various other national and private space organizations established colonies on Mars and the Saturn moon of Titan and using light-sail technology launched probes to Alpha Centauri, its closet solar neighbor. Global conflict in the middle of the 21st century slowed development of interstellar travel, but not before a tech startup built the first spaceships capable of traveling outside the solar system.

Now, several years after the establishment of diplomatic ties with The Cathari Alliance, Earth Secretary General Marsha Allen was deep in thought as she looked at a map of nearby space.

"What am I looking at?" asked the Secretary General.

"This is a map of the solar system. It indicates...," an aided started to say.

"I get what this is" snapped the Secretary General. "What I don't get is why I'm looking at it."

"Um...well..," began the aide. "This particular chart shows the location of all in system space vessels we are aware of."

"Nice. Now, I ask again, why am I looking at it?"

The flustered aid was relived when Chief Space Operations Commander, General Lin Cai interrupted. "Madam Secretary General," began the Chief, "this is important because of what it does not tell us."

Now more puzzled then informed, Secretary General Allen looked pointedly at General Cai before asking, "would you get to the point, please."

Not deterred, Cai continued, "it does not show the location of three unknown ships that we know, at least from previous intel, were parked near the orbit of Neptune. They seem to have vanished."

"Vanished...or went somewhere else," suggested Secretary General Allen.

"Vanished," said General Cai. "They are...gone."

AT A DISTANCE OF 2.9 BILLION MILES FROM Earth, the enormous ice giant Neptune orbited the sun slowly. While it takes Neptune 165 years to orbit the sun, it only takes a little more than four hours for light to travel between Earth and Neptune. Humans once relied on radio waves for communicating. It was a slow and tedious method and simply programming a Martian rover or an orbiting satellite could take days. Over time, humanity developed ever faster methods of communication. What communication once took hours to travel between planets, it could now be transferred almost instantly – at least inside the Solar System.

Three massive ships of the D'lai orbited Neptune for several weeks as they gathered intel on Earth and the various inhabited planets and moons. The D'lai grew more curious about Earth in recent years and regularly dispatched ships to observe. Humanity started to become a little more active with its neighbors, the Gathung, and so the D'lai stepped up their observations. They even went so far as to quietly visit the planet. The D'lai included the conquest of Earth as part of its long term objectives even before Earth was aware of its role in the galaxy. Humans were tenacious and the D'lai Authority believed they could mold them into their own image.

Neptune was the perfect spot to witness the distant space ports the humans built with the assistance of the Cathari Alliance and the Gathung. These space ports were busy hubs of activity with dozens of crafts passing in and out monthly on the way to or from neighboring systems.

The commanders of the D'lai ships did not bother to keep their cloaking devices active as they assumed that no humans or other species were near enough to gather usable data on their vehicles designs and origins. They were well aware that Earth detected them, they simply didn't care. The vast bulk of the D'lai fleet in the Sol system was cloaked well beyond Earth's moon. The three ships near Neptune were the bait to keep the humans off guard and looking in the wrong place.

Several years before Earth's final global conflict, humans reached beyond their own tiny planet and began to colonize other habitable planets in their system. Mars was the obvious choice for decades, but they also found the large moon of Titan to be an ideal location for exploration and growth. Together, the two colonies of Mars and Titan grew and became self-reliant. Each of the new worlds developed its own planetary systems and humans began to think of themselves as Martians or Titans. Most of the other species in the galaxy did not bother to colonize within their own systems and this intrigued the D'lai. What was different about humanity that they weren't content with just their home planet? The D'lai intended to use that innate curiosity against Earth in the very near future.

At about the same time as Negotiator D'iash was ordering her crew to travel to Cathar Prime, the commanders of the D'lai ships received orders from the D'lai Authority as well. However, the objectives were different. While D'iash was traveling to Cathar Prime to begin the first phase of the conquest, the three D'lai vessels in the Sol system were to move in closer to the space port orbiting the Saturn moon of Titan. These D'lai were the first line of intelligence if Earth and its xenophobic inhabitants started to ready themselves for possible interstellar altercations. It was widely feared that if Earth involved itself too heavily with other civilizations, the dynamics would shift too far for the D'lai to continue their plans. They did not yet realize that Earth prepared itself for years and it would soon become center stage in the coming conflict.

The risk in getting deeper into the Sol System, however was greater the closer to Earth. Therefore, a secondary objective of the D'lai commanders was to cloak themselves and rig for silent-running. The rest of the vast fleet kept itself hidden and it would do not good for humans to realize that an attack was imminent.

The D'lai quietly left the neighborhood of Neptune and began the short journey to orbit the moon Enceladus, near Saturn.

# CHAPTER 3

Ambassador Liuna was annoyed. Very annoyed. Her meeting with Gathung First Dictator Kwiu Zig did not go as planned. Not only had the First Dictator hid his illness from the leadership of the Cathari Alliance, the D'lai were getting more active.

"What exactly are they up to," the Ambassador said to herself as she paced her ceremonial office. "Why now?"

Her thoughts were disturbed when an aide paged her to notify her that the Security Minister and the Minister of Planetary Affairs were in the ante-chamber.

"Send them in."

The two ministers entered the spacious office and sat down in chairs near the Ambassador.

Liuna paused for a few heartbeats as she gathered her thoughts. Looking pointedly at each of the ministers, she began. "Ministers, I have discovered one...no two...disturbing facts.

The two ministers shifted nervously as Liuna continued. "First Dictator Zig is dying."

The Minister of Planetary Affairs looked up sharply. "What will happen on Gathung'l when he dies?"

"There are succession plans in his government. However, they don't call him *First* Dictator for no reason," Liuna replied.

"And the second fact Ambassador?" asked the Minister.

"The D'lai are increasing their activity in the Orion Arm," stated the Ambassador.

"What?" asked the Security Minister. "So not only is the Leader of Gathung'l dying, but his planet is once again endangered by the D'lai?"

"Not just his planet. Our planet."

Incredulous, both ministers shook their heads. "Yes," said Liuna, "that is how things *appear*. I believe there is more going on."

Ambassador Liuna picked up a small data device and showed it to the ministers. "I've received intelligence from Secretary General Allen of Earth that three ships were sighted near a planet in the Sol System. These three ships subsequently vanished."

The Security Minister sat up straighter in his chair. "The D'lai?"

Ambassador Liuna paused a moment before replying. "I believe so. I believe the D'lai are observing the humans. For what reason, I can only guess."

"A multi-front invasion," stated the Security Minister matter-of-factly. The room fell quiet for a long time.

"War," Liuna said. "Gentleman, the D'lai are about to invade. We must prepare. Now."

"We don't have much in the way of ground based weapons. If the D'lai come, we will have to rely on our orbital platforms," said the Security Minister.

"Let's review our defensive strategies. We should also alert the allies to send defensive ships," said Liuna.

"If the D'lai are preparing for war, perhaps we should also consider implementing our plans to reveal...," said the Minister of Planetary Affairs.

"Let me stop you right there, Minister," said Liuna, "we don't know what the D'lai have planned and revealing our historic shame can only make things worse."

"I believe the people deserve to know why the D'lai..."

"No. Let's see how things proceed first. We don't need to create problems, yet."

Liuna dismissed the two ministers and sat down heavily. She understood that her people had long forgotten the truth but revealing it when war possibly loomed only spelled disaster. How would she explain that for a thousand years their own government hid the darkest secret in Cathari history? Liuna shook the thought off and resumed reading her daily briefing.

GALLAGHER GREW MORE FRUSTRATED AS TIME went by. He could not determine how much time passed, but he was certain it several hours. The restraints were becoming more and more uncomfortable with each minute. Now, he needed to pee. Badly.

"Hello," he said hoping anyone was listening. "You can't keep me locked up like this forever."

He tried to pass the time reflecting on how he got here. Earlier today his only beef was with the First Engineer who ordered him to do grunt work in an environmental suit. Now here he was, held hostage by some unknown aliens, on some unknown ship, going to some unknown location. Frustrated wasn't a word he would use to describe his predicament. Incensed would be a better term.

Just as he figured he would have to relieve his bladder from the chair, he heard a soft *click* and the restraints on his arms and legs retracted back into the chair. He suddenly stood, rubbed his sore wrists, and gaped as a hole opened in the floor.

"It figures," he said to no one in particular. Not caring about being watched, he relieved himself fast before the aliens changed their minds and something more dreadful happened.

He only just finished when the door whooshed open and the first alien he met re-entered the room. "Follow me," said the alien. Gallagher reluctantly followed the unknown alien out of the room and into a long corridor.

Gallagher was surprised he was not restrained or in some other way restricted as he walked along behind his captor. The long walk in this oddly long passageway gave him time to detect a few more traits about his captors. The so-called negotiator he spoke too earlier was so wrapped up head to toe with that odd not-fabric he couldn't discern anything more than her overlarge eyes. This alien, despite only seeing his backside, gave Gallagher time to discern odd behaviors such as how he walked. Gallagher didn't think that the Negotiator and this fellow in front of him were the same species. The Negotiator was graceful. Even though this alien appeared bipedal, walking upright appeared like it was not quite natural. The mottled gray skin and lack of hair was, well … weird.

After what felt like minutes walking in this really long corridor with doors every few feet, the alien turned and motioned to an open door. Gallagher shrugged and walked in, surprised by the fact it appeared like these were some kind of crew quarters. Turning in confusion, he was about to ask the alien what the deal was when the door slid shut, leaving him alone. Gallagher detected no obvious method of opening the door, so he turned to study the new room. He observed what appeared to be a small eating area, a desk, and some kind of tiny, cramped bed. The best feature of the room and the one that gave Gallagher the most pleasure was a window. Being able to look out at the surrounding space made him feel a little less claustrophobic. It didn't really matter that all he saw was streaks of starry light as the ship traveled at faster than light speed.

"Well, at least I know we are still in space," Gallagher mused to himself. "Great."

Gallagher settled down in a very uncomfortable chair. He wondered if anyone aboard *The Avenger* missed him yet. Surely by now they noticed his disappearance. His thoughts were interrupted by the view out of his window. The star field slowly morphed, and he realized the ship was returning to normal space. He watched as a mammoth far off planet entered his field of vision. He recognized what he thought to be Cathar Prime. The last place he remembered being was in empty space nowhere near any major planets. His ship had been traveling at sub-light speed through the Ross 128 system after finishing a mission to Gathung'l. The plan was to head back to Saturn. Now, he was in another star system, a dozen light years from Earth.

"Why am I here!" This was infuriating. All Gallagher wanted was his bunk and a good meal. Being held captive on some alien ship with no idea why or what they planned was frustrating.

It is small wonder Gallagher almost missed the flashing icon on a wall console. It wasn't until the insistent beeping began he noticed it. He stood and walked over to the source of the noise, puzzled.

"What is this?"

Being unfamiliar with the alien technology onboard this ship, he figured it wouldn't hurt too much if he tried to silence it. He jabbed at a few indicators. He must have hit the correct one because a small holo-screen came into existence a few inches from the console and an alien face he didn't recognize materialized. Gallagher realized this alien was *similar* but not identical to the others he had seen.

"Whoa...buddy."

"Excuse my interruption *Dätëch*," the alien said, "please listen and don't react."

Gallagher nodded, curious.

"I can't speak to you in person because... um... I'm otherwise not able to get to your deck."

"Just what is going on buckaroo," began Gallagher. "I mean, you all haven't been accommodating."

The alien actually appeared to be nodding in agreement. "Apologies *Dätëch*. It is unavoidable. Our

Negotiator would put you out an airlock if she didn't have need of you."

"Now, that's not terribly friendly."

"Please...listen. You need to remember this..."

"Remember what? Why not tell me..."

"The D'lai are here."

With that, the holo-screen vanished, replaced by another blinking icon of an arrow pointing to the now open door.

"*Dätëch?* The D'lai? What does that mean?"

NAVIGATOR ARVESP ERTH SAT ALONE IN HER small quarters thinking over what happened earlier that day. Her day started normally with a shift on the bridge. She didn't expect to find herself in close combat with who she *thought* of as a friend, and then to be confined to her quarters as a result.

Arvesp pondered her predicament while she casually glanced at photos she kept on a nearby dresser. She had been raised on the Sumor continent of her home planet Gathung'l. A less than desired locale, Sumor was considered to be inferior to the much larger and dominant northern continent of

Naomor. Where the northern continent boasted great forests and sparse cities, the southern region was more of a desert. Consequently, its inhabitants were of darker skin and most of them had no hair on their bodies except a small patch on their heads.

Sumorians tended to live in small, nomadic tribes. Before the D'lai conquered the planet, they were more often than not used as laborers in the bigger Naomorian cities owing to their strong work ethics and sense of loyalty to their superiors. After the D'lai left Gathung'l and First Dictator Kwiu Zig rose to power, Sumor became more important to the overall global economy owing to the discovery of rich mineral deposits, which were essential to the building of ships to travel the stars. Arvesp's tribal village had been enriched by the growth of mining and industry which gave her the opportunity to study and to eventually join the crew of *The Avenger*.

Now, sitting in her quarters, she kept going over and over again in her head what happened. She wondered if she overreacted to Zika's attempt to flee the bridge and what the intruder alert meant. Her natural inclination to submit to anyone from Naomor, including Zika, made her second guess her reactions. However, Arvesp indeed did see Zika attempting to flee. That was an undeniable fact that her brain would not let her get past. However, despite knowing what she saw, she still hoped she was not wrong and this would not result in her being sent back to Gath-ung'l in disgrace. Her family depended on her income and status. Very few Sumorians enjoyed the distinc-tion of being an officer on a space ship and even fewer of them were female.

Now sitting alone in her quarters after all the earlier drama, she fretted and worried. Her leg was still sore from where the blaster bolt glanced off her. She made a mental note to wrap it in a bandage. The last thing she needed was an infection. It also upset Arvesp because she considered Zika a friend. She even once harbored hopes of something more between them. She hoped that her attraction was not misplaced. Zika had always been kind, and they often shared meals together. It wasn't unheard-of for a poor backwater My like herself to fall in love with a more cultured Ly like Zika. She shook herself to rid her brain of these thoughts. Zika attacked her. He didn't see her in the same way. The thought proved too sad to contemplate.

Her thoughts were interrupted by the sound of her comm panel alerting her to a message. She glanced at it and sat up straighter when she read it. Captain Ziqna ordered all officers to the bridge, herself included. Something was up. She slowly stood, adjusted her uniform, and left her quarters.

AFTER HUMANITY ENCOUNTERED THE CATHARI and figured out not only were they not alone, but a ton of civilizations existed in the galaxy, they began to focus even more heavily on two things: planetary defense and exploration. They began a major effort to clean up all the junk orbiting the planet while at the same time establishing outposts in what they imagined to themselves to be deep space, but was only their planetary neighbors. Other advanced civilizations would have perhaps laughed at the early feeble attempts to "get a grip" on what was going on in the galaxy, but humans were not noted for their understanding of the subtleties. They plowed ahead as humans tend to do, unaware and uncaring about how their actions affected the rest of the galaxy.

Earth already started large scale settlements on Mars and the moon of Titan by the time the aliens arrived, so planetary leaders worked to increase the human presence on those distant worlds. Plans were made to build a space hub out near Saturn with the belief it would be far enough away from the home world that any invading aliens would be detected long before arriving at Earth. Humans hadn't yet discovered faster than light travel and had no notions species like the D'lai possessed the technology to fold space. A trip for humans from Earth to Saturn once took many months before they too discovered improved methods of propulsion. A trip for the D'lai took mere hours. No amount of human planning and ingenuity prepared them for that reality. Earth was outmatched, but that didn't mean humans would lie down and take it. Humans had been quietly working with the Gathung on an advanced planetary defense system, and it was almost ready.

The three mysterious ships that had been sighted and then lost by Earth planetary defense forces made the journey from Neptune to Saturn and began a high orbit around Enceladus. The massive space hub near Titan currently hosted a dozen starships from multiple star systems. The largest ship at the space hub, a ship called *Voyager*, was an Earth ship. The name was inspired by the historic missions that once were the planets only foray into interstellar space.

*Voyager* boasted a crew of one hundred humans and was capable of traveling from the Sol System to Alpha Centauri in two days. Other ships at the space hub were smaller. None of them were aware of the lurking D'lai nearby.

Onboard *Voyager* Captain Kelly Pryce sat on the ships spacious bridge reading over reports of nearby space traffic. At 49, she became the first female ships captain to take command of *Voyager* since it launched ten years earlier. She beamed with pride of her accomplishments and bristled at comparisons made of her with other women. Raised on Mars, Captain Pryce was a self-starter and an out of the box thinker. While she ordinarily a stickler for the rules and procedures of life aboard a ship, she found subtle ways around those same rules and procedures if it furthered her goals or her career. The current mission of *Voyager* was to shuttle a human ambassador to a summit meeting on Cathar Prime. Captain Pryce felt the mission to be too dull for Earth's preeminent ship but orders were orders. It would give her some time to fine tune some other pressing issues onboard the ship.

"Captain, we have received permission to undock," said the Comms Officer from his station near the navigator.

"Navigator, undock and proceed at half speed," ordered the Captain. "Let's make sure to steer clear of all this traffic before we engage our FTL drive."

"Aye Captain," said the Navigator matter-of-factly. "Undocking in process."

Captain Pryce resumed reading the reports. Earlier that morning she welcomed the Ambassador and made the usual pleasantries. "I sure hope this trip is worth the trouble," she said to herself afterwards.

Undocking from the space hub was a delicate maneuver that took time. With all the congestion of nearby ships, it would take more than an hour for *Voyager* to fully undock and get far enough away from Titan and the gravity well of Saturn to engage the FTL drive. Traveling faster than light required a ship to be in open space. The gravity of a massive planet like Saturn caused anomalies with course plotting that the early FTL attempts discovered with devastating clarity.

One early attempt at FTL space flight resulted in the entire ship breaking apart, killing the dozen crew members aboard. Scientists over time adjusted their schematics and theories and later attempts proved more successful. The first ever successful FTL flight from the Sol System to Alpha Centauri had been a major success in humanity's desire to "just get out there." That flight cut the light speed travel time from just over four years down to three weeks. Humans understood if they wanted to be a major force in the galaxy, this would need to be improved. Now it was standard to travel one light year every 12 hours.

*Voyager* just entered a safe flight zone when warning lights began erupting from multiple consoles and work stations. Captain Pryce worked feverishly to determine the cause. There were no charted gravity sources within acceptable ranges but that didn't prevent the ship from detecting three of them nearby.

"All stop!"

The ship stopped its forward momentum. "Someone tell me what the hell is going on," ordered the Captain.

After a few seconds, the crew member manning the tactical station reported, "the ships sensors detected three small gravity wells in close proximity to our flight path."

"What is the status of them? What are they?"

"Unknown Captain. We can detect them but we can't see them."

Captain Pryce realized that could only mean there were cloaked ships out there. She understood many other races they encountered possessed cloaking technology but all of them at least pretended they never used them inside a planetary system.

The three D'lai ships had been detected waited quietly to see how the human ship would react. They did not anticipate *Voyager* would make its flight path so close to them and the sheer size of the D'lai ships meant their gravity would easily be detected by passing ships. The commander of the lead ship made a snap decision. His orders were to maintain observation of the humans and avoid detection. He knew a ship passing so close would not only detect them but would likely report that detection back to their command. He was also a hot-head and grew angry at being relegated to a minor role in the D'lai's long term strategic plans. He presumed a ship blowing up wouldn't necessarily lead to a belief of alien intervention. He didn't take into account how Earth would react because the D'lai hadn't studied humans long enough.

"Weapons. Destroy that ship," he ordered.

Without any warning of impending doom or the means to protect itself, *Voyager* blew apart, scattering debris and corpses over a wide area of space.

Minutes after the destruction of *Voyager*, General Cai barged into Secretary General Allen's outer office. He had no intention of waiting for an appointment or even the usual pleasantries with Allen's staff. Instead, he stormed straight for her inner office, brushing past security agents and frantic staffers.

Allen had always been an efficient worker. Each day she began by reviewing the dozens of communications and briefings that came across her desk. She always paid particular attention to anything that talked about aliens. She had been intrigued when the Cathari first showed up in orbit and even though she had not herself had the opportunity to travel off world, she fervently hoped that one day she'd get that opportunity. She was mid way through a particularly dull scientific document when her secretary buzzed. Allen reached for the button but before she could even respond, her door banged open and in walked General Lin Cai.

General Cai was a disciplinarian and usually very stiff and formal. His father had been a high ranking official in the Chinese Communist Party and the

National People's Congress and was on track to become party chairman when the aliens arrived. Cai was not one prone to hysterics so the fact that he seemed in such a hurry seriously worried Secretary General Allen.

Allen glanced up from her desk. "Cai...what the..."

"Madam Secretary General. Our long range ship *Voyager* was just destroyed near Saturn.

The Secretary General stood. "What? How?"

Several high level aides followed General Cai into the spacious office. "We received two transmissions seconds before the ship disappeared from our screens," began the General. "The first was a detection of three small gravity wells near their FTL injection coordinates."

"And the second?"

The General pointed at an aide. "Play the transmission," he ordered.

The aide nodded and pressed an icon on his pad. The room went quiet as they listened.

No voices were intelligible. The only sound was the sound of numerous voices screaming and then all at once cut off.

The office remained quiet for several seconds before Allen interrupted the stillness. "No."

Men and women began rushing in and out of the office, presumably engaging in frenetic activity as a result of the dire news. The Secretary General slumped in her chair and looked at Chief of Space Operations Cai.

"What now?"

"First, ma'am, we need to ascertain what happened exactly," the General stated.

"Do you think this disaster has anything to do with the three missing ships from Neptune?"

"Most likely. We do know there were three gravity wells where there shouldn't have been any. The ships we detected near Neptune were quite huge and most definitely had enough mass."

"Who are they, General?" The Secretary General looked at a message on her console for a moment, then looked back up. "Do we have any idea? Are they listed sentients?"

"At this time we do not have any intelligence on origins, ma'am."

"Then perhaps we better get some, so we know if this was an accident or an act of war."

"Where are we in developing our planetary shields?"

Cai thought for a moment. "The prototype is ready for deployment. It is currently onboard *The Avenger,* on its way back from Gathung'l.

"Get that ship back ASAP. We might need it soon,"

The General nodded his head and turned to leave.

"Oh, and General," began Allen. The General turned to face her. "Act quickly."

General Lin Cai nodded tersely and strolled adamantly from the room.

Secretary General Allen began running over a list of things to do in her head. At the top of her list was notifying the Cathari Ambassador the representative from Earth would not be coming after all. She also decided she needed to call her sister to check in.

"It's been too long," she mumbled to herself, "and not yet long enough."

BACK ON *THE AVENGER,* ZIKA UKU SAT IN THE cramped holding cell and worried. The Gathung were not known for their love of aesthetics and this brig was no exception. Zika's quarters had been cramped and small but this cell was tiny. He barely had enough room to turn around in and it possessed only a chair, a cot, and one tiny shelf that would not hold more than one bottle or cup.

He realized now he should have kept his cool when the ship was attacked, but he panicked. He *knew* what the sudden power loss meant even if no one else did. He remembered the D'lai would capture smaller vessels, send agents aboard to gather data, and release the ships with no real damage done. What he didn't know was why the D'lai would be interested in *The Avenger*. Zika was not briefed on the planet cloaking tech that was onboard. To his knowledge, the ship was merely a glorified shuttle between Gathung'l and Earth.

Back on Gathung'l, he prepared for this routine mission by reading secretly obtained mission briefs of other Gathung ships. He trained to keep his head down and do his duty to avoid detection. The simple fact was almost every Gathung ship included a D'lai spy aboard. The other simple fact was almost no one *knew* there was a spy on board. Zika screwed up and he recognized his mission was likely over if he couldn't come up with a damned good reason why he fired on Arvesp on the bridge.

"Why *did* I fire?" He pondered aloud. "I mean, why!" Zika racked his brain for answers. After a few moments, he had an idea. What if he told the truth. What if he told Captain Ziqna all about the infiltration and the actions of the D'lai, all of it. It was worth a shot.

Surely Ziqna would understand. He had been on Gathung'l during the occupation and new all about the cruelty and the manipulation of the D'lai. Zika didn't really know what kind of life the Captain had back then, though. Maybe Ziqna would react badly. Zika felt fear rising once more at the thought of coming clean.

He screwed up his courage and shook his head to clear it. Ziqna would understand. He had to! Zika had only acted the way he did to save his own family. Before his resolve could weaken, he stood and worked to calm his nerves and his facial expression. Approaching the bars of his cell, he called to the security guard manning the small holding area.

"Let the Captain know I'm ready to talk," Zika said.

The guard actually snorted before replying,

"Sure. I'll do that," returning his attention to his pad.

"I'm still your superior officer," shouted Zika. "Do it!"

Grumbling, the guard looked at Zika for a long moment, then typed a brief message on his pad.

Zika sat back down. His experience with the Captain made him aware Ziqna would not be able to resist finding out what was happening on his ship. He didn't know how long it would be, but he hoped the Captain would come. All he had to do now was wait, and figure out how much truth he was willing to reveal.

"Only enough to keep from getting killed," he said to no one in particular.

# CHAPTER 4

The First Dictator sat in a comfortable chair on his shuttle. He was exhausted from his meeting with the other planetary leaders over the past six hours. The Plenary Session of the Cathari Alliance was necessary to keep the various members working together. However, since he was also aware of a growing threat from the D'lai, the squabbling over which planet should obtain certain space lane rights seemed less than relevant.

After his revelation with Ambassador Liuna prior to the Plenary Session, he was tempted to reveal his knowledge, but he was afraid that not only would the disclosure completely disrupt the unity of the Alliance but that any spies among the planetary leaders and their innumerable aides would create more problems than they needed at the moment. Kwiu Zig had no direct proof or knowledge of spies, but he understood the D'lai and how they manipulated events unwitnessed. He spent years rebuilding his own civilization after their disastrous occupation.

An aide bowed and then entered the First Dictator's quarters. "Pardon me Sir," the aide began. "We have received an intercept from Earth."

Kwiu Zig grunted. "What intercept?" He was not in the mood to hear about the petty humans and their less than important problems.

"Sir, the humans are not aware but we suspect the D'lai have been operating in their space." The aide was going to continue when he was interrupted.

"The D'lai, in *human* space?"

"Yes Sir. One of the human ships was destroyed after intercepting three invisible gravity wells."

"The humans have cloaking technology," he said. "Why do we believe this was not them?"

"We have no direct evidence and the humans have no experience with the D'lai."

Kwiu Zig thought for a few moments. "And what of our own *agents* in the Sol System?"

The aide flushed for a moment before responding.

"Sir, one of our agents was *onboard* their ship."

The First Dictator shook his head in disbelief. "Leave. I must think of next steps."

The aide bowed deeper than the first time as he backed swiftly out of the room. The First Dictator sighed and sank deeper into his seat. The news was not good and it only reinforced his own fears of a rising D'lai threat throughout the entire region. He pressed an icon on his pad.

"Sir?" The voice on the other end responded instantly.

"Get in touch with Ambassador Liuna. Tell he we need to meet. Again." Zig switched off the console and sat back, trying to rest a little before the next crisis.

GALLAGHER PUZZLED OVER THE INDICATORS suggesting he should walk out of the room he was currently in. The alien who spoke to him suggested he should "follow the indicators." Gallagher shrugged, figuring nothing worse would happen to him and so he carefully stepped outside of the room. Further down the long corridor was another flashing sign.

"Okay, so he left me some bread crumbs."

Gallagher cautiously followed the signals, surprised that he encountered no other aliens on his way. After he passed maybe fifteen closed doors, he came upon an open door. Shrugging again, he entered the room. At once, the door closed shut behind him. Gallagher thought at first that this was an elaborate trap to trick him to go into an even more restrictive environment. This room, however, was different. Room wasn't quite the correct word. This looked like something far more useful.

"Escape pods."

One final indicator light was flashing on an open hatch in the center of the room. Hoping that his escape in an escape pod wouldn't be the last thing he ever did, Gallagher got inside the shockingly small ship, attempted to strap himself in, and waited. The seats were not quite right for a human frame so he did his best.

Nothing.

Gallagher looked around. "I don't read their language," he said to no one. He raised his voice, hoping someone would overhear him. "Hey, I don't read whatever this is." A few seconds went by and then a soft whoosh sound off to his left and another indicator light. The hatch to the pod closed and he braced himself. If this escape pod was anything like what Earth developed, he was in for a wild ride. Gallagher was thankful when the pod departed the ship smoothly, and automatically oriented itself toward the planet.

From this vantage point in space, Gallagher studied the ship he was currently fleeing. The ship hadn't yet re-engaged its cloak after returning to normal space and he wondered why. Surely they would not want to be detected by the Cathari. Would they? He realized with sudden clarity that these aliens, whoever they were, wanted to be seen. They were actively intimidating the Cathari. He could only guess at their reasons but it did feel ominous to him.

From what he caught glimpses of out the small porthole, it was a monster of a ship. Human and alien designs of space ships were different. Human design tended to mimic what television producers had envisioned ages ago. Obviously these aliens had never seen Star Trek or Star Wars so their designs were a jumble and were visually odd to him.

"I guess if you don't want someone to target your bridge, don't make it so obvious where it is," Gallagher said.

A few seconds later the escape pod re-oriented itself and the ship vanished. He half expected that his flight would end in fire and death, but quite the opposite occurred. His secret benefactor must have kept the escape pod off the massive ships sensors and after a short flight, he entered the planetary atmosphere. Once his escape pod was through the atmosphere of Cathar Prime, the sudden g forces slammed him against the bulkhead. After what felt like an eternity, he realized the pod was slowing and the ground outside the small porthole was rapidly rising. The escape pod landed softly in a field as the outer door blew off. Gallagher tentatively stepped outside the pod, looked around and froze. Four outsized and uniformed Cathari were surrounding him. He did what any human would do. He raised his arms in surrender.

"Take me to your leader," he said in half jest and half seriousness. Noting the stern looks of his would be captors, he added, "please."

AMBASSADOR LIUNA WAS DEEP IN DISCUSSION with the First Dictator when a message popped up on her screen. She was about to swipe it away when she recognized the word "human" and "escape pod."

"One moment Kwiu," she stated. "I need to take a message."

The First Dictator grunted as Liuna read the message. It seems that a human, Major Cormac Gallagher, just landed on Cathar Prime in an escape pod.

"Kwiu, I need to get back to you."

"Wait a moment. You don't understand. The D'lai are *here*," said Zig.

"Yes, and so are the humans."

Kwiu Zig's face contorted in confusion. "I thought their ambassador was killed."

"Yes, but somehow another one has shown up outside the capital city."

Kwiu Zig twisted in his seat and looked over his shoulder. Liuna didn't understand what he said to a nearby aide. He turned back to the monitor.

"I know of this human and his mission. We need to meet with that human," he said. "Together."

Ambassador Liuna sighed impatiently. "Fine. One hour then."

She switched off the screen as Zig nodded his agreement.

She sat back in her chair and thought over matters for a time. Just when things looked to be going right for the Alliance and her planet, here came the Gathung with their dire warnings of impending doom. It seemed every few years some crisis or another was brought to her attention by Alliance worlds. Gathung'l was understandably wary but she found no real reason for panic. It had been a lifetime since the D'lai left. Why would they come back now? What would be their purpose? Liuna batted away her concern. What had happened between Cathar Prime and the D'lai was hundreds of years in the past. Surely that was not the reason for their stepped up activity.

Liuna sat up straight as she thought of one really good reason for a sudden interest in galactic politics. She heard unverified reports recently that Earth and Gathung'l were involved in some super secret project. She understood from her studies and visits to both worlds that the two civilizations had violent pasts. Earth's past was quite a bit more recent, but she long thought they were moving beyond that. Could they be planning something that competed with the goals of the Alliance? It was true that Earth was not a full member, but Liuna worked tirelessly for the past few years to bring them fully on board. She intimately understood that Earth wasn't too keen on giving up its bristling planetary defenses but other than the D'lai, who hadn't really been seen or heard from in decades, there was no recognizable threat. A planet over-flowing with more defensive systems than were really appropriate just didn't sit well with the overly peaceful Cathari.

She pulled up the old reports of Gathung-Earth cooperation and reviewed them hastily. She under-stood she should be arranging to bring the human for her meeting with Kwiu Zig, but she put that aside for a few moments. She was looking for one particular fact that was dancing at the edge of her memory. Frus-trated, she gave up and ordered her security forces to bring the human into the capital. She then decided to take a few minutes and calm her roiling mind down with a short meditation cycle. That should help. She hoped.

GALLAGHER WAS NOT HAVING ALL THAT GREAT OF a day. After escaping the alien ship he now realized was D'lai, he was now being escorted through a series of buildings and open air plazas on his way to somewhere he only guessed at. He was grateful that his new captors appeared friendly. He'd had many interactions with the Cathari from his time living on planet so he would have been stunned if they had treated him badly. They were so peaceful they wouldn't voluntarily kill a stupid fly buzzing around their heads.

"Did they even have flies on Cathar Prime?" Gallagher laughed at his own question. His guards looked at him and just kept walking.

"Probably think I'm crazy."

The city, which he recognized as the capital of Cathar, was breathtaking. Each building and park seemed designed with the word *tranquility* in mind. Rising white spires, huge open green spaces, and smoothly flowing air and ground traffic filled the windows of the transport. His home world was not quite so nice to look at. Sure, cities like New York and London had their appeal, but he'd never quite seen such peaceful organization like this before.

He was about to turn and talk to his escorts when the air transport began to descend to ground level. He decided to wait and ask questions until he was with someone who was more *in charge* than these fellows were. At the same time, his curiosity was burning him up and he ached to unleash a rapid fire of questions just so he could gain a sense of not only *where* he was but *why* he was here at all.

The transport landed in a plaza decorated with what looked like hundreds of statues, each one placed in what would only be described as well organized chaos. He was so wrapped up in looking at the jumble of them he didn't notice that his escorts were trying to get him to leave the transport. Gallagher was startled as he realized that these Cathari would not actually lay a hand on him or restrain him in any way. It was madness to a human that a civilization as advanced as this wouldn't even handcuff an interloper on their planet.

He stood and followed who he figured to be the leader through an arched entryway. The room he now stepped into was vast. The ceiling rose high above them with huge windows that looked to be not only transparent but porous. He felt a slight breeze even while standing in front of one of them. The room was filled with plants and growing things of all shapes and sizes. Once again he found himself being awed by his surroundings and not noticing the movement of the beings near him.

After a minute or two, he watched as a tall, elegant Cathari woman approached him. Her flowing blue and gold garments were breathtaking and so perfectly wrapped her body as to seem to almost be a part of it. Gallagher couldn't detect her emotions as she approached. He assumed she had to be friendly. She was after all a Cathari. She reminded him of the Negotiator but he pushed that aside. These two could not be related at all. One was overly peaceful and the other was downright rude. However, he cautioned himself to not be fooled by her exterior. Humans long suspected the Cathari were friendly on the outside and scheming on the inside.

Once she got closer, she motioned to a small sitting area nearby. They both sat across from each other and Gallagher was just about to launch into his questions when he spied a group of Gathung approaching from another entrance. He frowned at them. The Gathung in the middle was *old*. He'd never seen one quite this ancient. All at once, he recognized the guy. Startled, he paid more attention and realized what was going on.

"So, the Ambassador of Cathari herself wants to meet with me, a lowly human?"

The Ambassador actually laughed at his

comment. "Not just that Ambassador," she began. "The First Dictator of Gathung is here as well."

Gallagher was puzzled. "Ambassador, I'm only a Major..."

"Yes, the human we were expecting was killed. We will treat you as an ambassador in his place."

"That's kind but..."

"Liuna," growled Kwiu Zig as he approached. "I don't wish to waste time."

The Ambassador swept her arms broadly to indicate the available seating and waited as the ancient Gathung leader settled himself down in a king-sized chair.

Liuna turned to Gallagher. "Now, let's talk about why you are here and what it is you want."

Gallagher settled in. This was going to take some time.

ENGINEER COREY HODGES WAS REVIEWING external video trying to figure out not only what happened during the mysterious power outages this morning, but also what happened to his friend and Second Engineer. It was worrisome that he had no clue what happened. *The Avenger* was important to the security of Earth and he didn't want anything to interfere with that.

"Dammit." Hodges saw on the feed where Gallagher was, then at the precise moment of the outage, the video cut out. He forwarded the feed and after a few minutes, when the feed returned, Gallagher wasn't there anymore.

Hodges sighed. Gallagher must have been killed or lost during the event. He was about to click off the video feed and froze. Rewinding, he paused at the precise moment when the feed ended. No, it didn't end. It just changed.

"Oh my God." Hodges burst from his seat and ran to the bridge.

Seconds later, he ran onto the bridge and ran straight into a bulkhead trying to avoid a crewman going the opposite direction. The same Scree crewman who had been creamed by Captain Ziqna earlier shrieked once more and flattened itself against the wall.

"Sorry bud." Hodges yelled over his shoulder as he looked frantically for the Captain.

Spotting Ziqna near the tactical station, he rushed over.

"Captain!"

Captain Ziqna turned around and groaned. "What is it Engineer?"

In response, Hodges pushed the tactical officer aside and pulled up the video feed on the console. He scrubbed forward to the point he had been at on his office computer.

"Look. What do you see?" Hodges asked.

The Captain looked and was about to say there was just a black field when he paused, looked closer and squinted.

"That is the inside of a ship. It looks like a cargo bay."

"It is a cargo bay," replied Hodges. "The only problem is, that isn't *our* cargo bay."

Captain Ziqna was confused. "Why are you showing this to me?"

Hodges zoomed in closer. "That cargo bay is *outside* our ship. It was surrounding our entire hull. That feed is an outside view of the ship at the moment we lost power and gravity."

"We were *inside* another ship?" Ziqna paled. "Who has the technology to do *that*?"

Even as he was asking the question, Ziqna feared the answer to his own question.

"The D'lai." Ziqna whirled and walked toward his command chair. "It is the D'lai. I have to notify Gathung Command at once."

At the mention of the D'lai, every Gathung in earshot felt dread filling them up from head to toe. They all secretly hoped the scourge of the D'lai was a distant memory and they would never again have to experience that civilization disrupting force.

Hodges didn't know much about the D'lai except they once occupied Gathung'l. If they were active in this region of space, that would not be good.

"The D'lai – if that is who they are – captured us and searched our records. They invaded our secrecy! If they found what we've been doing..." Ziqna trailed off.

Hodges nodded. The secret technology being developed by Earth and Gathung'l was critical and a very deeply held secret between the two worlds. If a hostile species were to stop them before its deployment, the past fifteen months of work would be for nothing.

"Hodges, go find out as much as you can about that other ship," said the Captain. "I have to contact Gathung'l."

Hodges agreed and returned to his office in Engineering. Ziqna departed the bridge and went to his private quarters. He had to be alone when he contacted his superiors. He didn't know how they would react and the very last thing he needed was for his own crew to be so frozen in fear they could not operate. Beside that, not everyone was briefed on the cloaking technology and he couldn't risk spies overhearing him.

After composing his report and sending it off, he paused for a moment and then wrote a much more private message to his family on Gathung'l. He expected that they would not reveal the contents of what he was about to share, but he wanted to make sure if things did get much worse, they at least would be as safe as possible.

Ziqna very much remembered the last occupation of the D'lai. His family had suffered. He would do everything in his power to prevent that from happening again.

GALLAGHER CROSSED HIS ARMS AS HE WAITED TO find out what was going on. The Cathari and Gathung leaders peered at him intently. Speaking with *any* planetary leader was way above Gallagher's pay grade, so he had no intention of starting this particular conversation. He didn't have to wait long.

"Human, why are you on Cathar Prime?" Liuna asked. Liuna was well aware of Gallagher's role onboard *The Avenger* and his time spent studying on Cather Prime.

"Well, it beats being on the D'lai ship."

Liuna reacted as if she had been slapped. "D'lai? Explain!" Liuna feared the D'lai more than even the Gathung. She knew the dark history between their two peoples and she struggled to remain calm even as her mind was racing in turmoil.

Gallagher explained how he had been minding his own business, doing some grunt work outside his ship near Gathung'l when he'd been captured, interrogated, forced to relieve himself in a hole in the ground, then blown off the ship in a tiny escape pod after the unexpected help of someone on board. Ambassador Liuna and the First Dictator listened intently. Liuna didn't understand.

"How do you know it was a D'lai ship?"

"They told me," replied Gallagher. "I mean, *one* of them told me."

He described how he had been led to the escape

pod bay, how the alien told him what was going on. Liuna's hand shot to her neck in fear.

"Did you *see* any of the D'lai?"

"I'm not sure," said Gallagher. "The one who called herself the Negotiator was covered head to toe but some shorter dudes looked, well, alien."

Liuna allowed herself to breath again. If Gallagher had not seen a member of the D'lai species, he could not guess at the hidden truth.

"What else did they tell you, Major," Liuna asked.

"Oh, right, he told me to tell the Cathari the D'lai were here."

First Dictator listened and pondered. "Human..." he began.

"Gallagher."

"Gallagher," continued Zig, "you are an engineer onboard *The Avenger*?"

Gallagher shrugged. "Yeah. Why?"

Kwiu Zig paused for an uncomfortably long time before continuing.

"Liuna, I need to come clean."

Liuna turned toward the First Dictator. "What do you mean Kwiu?"

A coughing spell temporarily halted Zig from

replying. A worried aide rushed up to him and Zig waved him away.

"This human knows what has been happening between Earth and Gathung'l."

The Ambassador shifted uncomfortably in her seat. "What is happening between your two worlds?"

"As you know, the Gathung are terrified of the D'lai. The Humans are pretty much terrified of everyone else."

Ambassador Liuna waved her hand in frustration. "What is the point?"

The First Dictator cleared his throat. "Earth and Gathung'l have been developing a device that will..." Kwiu Zig's eyes went wide as Gallagher jumped from his seat and leaped across the short distance. "What the..."

Gallagher tackled both the Ambassador and the First Dictator a millisecond before an enormous explosion rocked the atrium. Intense heat and debris scorched the room. Thanks to the quick actions of Major Gallagher, the three of them found themselves to be safe behind toppled furniture they had been sitting on only a second earlier.

The First Dictator moaned in pain. "Get off me human!"

Gallagher lifted himself up, looked around tentatively, then lowered himself back to the ground, right next to the old Gathung leader. "Don't move," Gallagher whispered. Another explosion rocked the room. Everyone instinctively covered their heads. Ambassador Liuna squealed and Gallagher thought she was actually crying, when in reality a piece of shrapnel was sticking out of her leg. He came close to vomiting at the sight of her yellow blood.

He assessed the situation. Keeping low to the ground, he peered around the scorched furniture. Several charred and dismembered bodies were nearby. The explosion that rocked the room had been massive enough to blow an enormous hole in the outer wall. Gallagher noticed what looked like the same aliens from the D'lai ship running away from the blast. He was about to say something when he saw Cathari security forces responding and he waved them over to their location. The planetary leaders were whisked away as medics tended to their wounds and everyone around babbled and shouted. Gallagher stood and looked around the destroyed room.

"Now where do I go?" He asked to no one in particular. He didn't have long to wait.

## CHAPTER 5

The office of the Secretary General was chaotic. Aides, governmental ministers, and legislators were coming and going in quick succession. On top of all that, world leaders were calling. Everyone wanted to be told what was going on. Everyone was demanding precious time she would not devote. It was imperative the planetary government got the crisis under control. Secretary General Allen needed to have details on who destroyed *Voyager*, why they did it, and what that meant for the future.

It was also critical she get in touch with Gathung'l to ascertain the status of the Planetary Cloaking project. Allen was worried some kind of hostilities were about to break out. While Earth spent trillions in preparing itself for such an eventuality, there were gaps in their preparedness. Earth had lots of ideas but not enough of the technical competence to build an impenetrable planetary defense. Gathung'l, on the other hand, was far more superior technologically and shared a similar fear of outside alien civilizations. The only difference being Earth had never been invaded by aliens, unlike Gathung'l.

Weapons were useful if you saw an enemy coming but they weren't so helpful if you couldn't. Allen was well aware other civilizations possessed the ability to hide themselves with cloaking devices. Earth was one of the few worlds that refused to give up that ability. When the Cathari first began diplomacy with the planet, one of their first *demands* was they agree to never cloak their ships while traveling through a star system. The leaders of the planet at the time thought they was crazy. Who understood just what was out there and why announce yourself if you didn't have to? This was one of the main reasons why Earth had not joined the Cathari Alliance. Earth didn't trust other civilizations to always have Earth's best interests. Most humans didn't trust each other enough for very similar reasons.

Secretary General Allen entered the briefing room where her top military and political advisors were huddled around an expansive star map. She strolled purposely over to the group.

"Report."

Chief of Space Operations Lin Cai looked up. "Ma'am, we don't have a record of where the three missing ships are. We know they were near the Saturn Space Port, but we don't have the ability to detect them unless we are close enough to pick up their gravity."

"What is the status of *The Avenger*?" We need to know where the cloak is.

The General checked a status board. "The ship is heading to the system and should be arriving at Saturn within hours."

"And the Planetary Cloaking prototype?"

"According to our engineers onboard, the prototype is functional. They plan on conducting a functional test within the next few days."

Intelligence Minister Perla Costa interrupted. "Ma'am, our agents on board *The Avenger* have informed us a D'lai ship intercepted and boarded them as they were traveling here."

"D'lai? Isn't that the same aliens that enslaved the Gathung?"

"Yes, Ma'am," continued Minister Costa. "*The Avenger* experienced system wide power failure and temporary loss of artificial gravity. Their systems indicated the ship had been boarded and further investigation suggested a much larger ship took *The Avenger* inside its hangar bay."

"What makes us think the D'lai did this?" Allen asked.

"Well, we don't know that conclusively," said Minister Perla. "What we do know is Captain Ziqna reported to his commanders it was the D'lai. He was quite panicked."

Secretary General Allen paused in thought. Turning back to General Cai, she said, "General. Is it safe to bring the prototype online so near where *Voyager* was destroyed? What if these D'lai are watching?"

"You are right Ma'am, I don't think we want them to see us deploy it. The whole idea is to keep it as a *secret* weapon. What good would it do if everyone knew about it?"

"Precisely. Let's develop a plan to deploy it a little more secretly."

"Agreed," said the General.

General Cai and Minister Costa walked over to a group of officers to develop a contingency plan while the Secretary General conferred with others in the room. After a short time, the group reassembled. Allen listened as Cai and the others outlined a plan to test the prototype while remaining as quiet and unobtrusive about it as possible.

"Notify Gathung Command and update the plans."

She hoped this would work. They couldn't afford to let the whole galaxy know what they were up to. She was pretty sure the Cathari wouldn't like it and she definitely didn't want anyone else to know. Not yet at least.

AFTER EARTH LEADERS FORMULATED THEIR PLAN and consulted with Gathung'l, updated orders had been sent to *The Avenger*. They were ordered to make all speed to the Sol System and enter orbit around Jupiter. Unusually, they were also ordered to cloak and remain so until further orders were given. The Captain made the appropriate orders to his bridge crew. Ziqna relished the opportunity to flaunt Alliance protocols and fly silently.

About the same time he received his orders from Gathung, he also received word from the holding cells that Security Officer Zika wanted to speak with him. Captain Ziqna wanted desperately to get to the bottom of all the morning's nonsense before they arrived on station at Jupiter.

Upon entering the holding area, the Captain approached Zika. He didn't say anything to the Security Officer but his commanding presence was all Zika needed to begin spilling out all his secrets.

"Captain, I don't know you well enough to know how you will react," began Zika. "I'm a...spy... for the D'lai."

That was all Captain Ziqna needed to hear. He roared in anger as he whirled to a nearby officer. "Get this traitor *off* my ship!"

Zika began protesting loudly. "Captain...I have reasons..."

The Captain didn't hear nor did he care what Zika said. Gathung justice was as swift as it was brutal. They learned from the D'lai. Zika was whisked away, screaming down a corridor, as the Captain followed. The security officer manhandling Zika flung him into a small enclosed space. Zika screamed in terror as he realized he was in an exterior airlock.

Turning to the enraged Captain, the security officer indicated the control panel on the outside of the airlock. Without hesitation or showing any level of remorse, he entered his pass code and a countdown timer began. Ten seconds later, a small outer hatch opened and Zika was blown into the vacuum of space, his screams cut off as the oxygen in his lungs froze.

Ziqna turned to the impassive officer. "You're in charge now. Get me everything you can find about him."

Captain Ziqna stormed off back to the bridge.

AMBASSADOR LIUNA RECLINED IN A BED AS SHE received reports from her staff about the explosions that interfered with her meeting with the human and the First Dictator. Her medical doctors removed a jagged piece of metal from her leg but other than some pain, she was no worse for the wear. The Gathung leader wasn't in as good shape as she was. Liuna worried this disaster would leave the Gathung people leaderless at a time when they could ill afford it.

Liuna read report after report of what happened during her meeting. She was most distressed by the fact that the peace of her home world had been shattered by the attack. It was not yet known what happened, but it was quite obvious someone or something didn't want her talking to the human and the First Dictator.

Liuna checked the time on her pad before rubbing her eyes tiredly. She should delegate and allow her subordinates to get to the bottom of this whole mess, but she had no intention of letting this go and relaxing, despite what her doctors tersely suggested. She needed to know what happened and why.

What was it Kwiu was about to tell her? He started to talk about this super secret project he was involved in with Earth. Liuna figured it probably was some kind of defensive program. After all, the Gathung were deathly afraid of being reconquered. She understood this and empathized with them.

However, it had been so long since there had been any real threat to any of the Cathari Alliance civilizations. Why would that change? She began to suspect with the involvement of Earth, the delicate balance she and her predecessors tried to strike in this region of the galaxy was unraveling. She wasn't sure why that would be the case, but the initial experiences with Earth had been less than satisfying.

When the Cathari first came upon the Sol System and Earth in particular, much discussion occurred in the upper echelons of the Alliance about whether the humans were ready for contact. It was common knowledge Earth had been visited numerous times by various races of aliens but none of them made what was termed *First Contact*. Most of the visitations had been to gather intelligence on the planet and, admittedly, some of it was just for fun. While the Cathari themselves never visited Earth, others did. It annoyed the Alliance but they couldn't stop the more curious and playful civilizations from their misbehavior.

Once First Contact was formally made, the Cathari reeled in almost universal horror at the reaction of the inhabitants. They contacted dozens of other planetary civilizations and *none* reacted the way the humans did. Overnight, mass chaos erupted on the planet. To the Cathari way of thinking, this chaos had nothing to do with the sudden appearance of enormous space ships in orbit and visible from the ground. Humans didn't react at all the way it was expected they would. The Cathari decided to withdraw, which only created more problems globally.

Their sudden presence did have the effect of spurring unification efforts among the various nations. However, humanity didn't unify because it felt like it was time for all the disparate nations to come together in love and harmony and holding hands and all that nonsense. They united because now, to humans way of thinking, there was a serious threat. They didn't realize the threat was *not* from the Cathari.

Liuna had been with the initial expedition that contacted Earth. She was part of the diplomatic corps so she had been privy to the discussion about withdrawal and any follow-up. She remembered pitying the inhabitants of the Earth who up until that point were unaware there were other sentient life forms in the galaxy. The Cathari civilization evolved the way it did *because* they were aware of other civilizations.

Liuna and the other diplomats of the dozen or so other ships were in constant contact as they observed from a distance how Earth reacted to their presence.

Liuna's ship was dispatched to monitor the developments and reactions on Mars. She was grateful at least here, humans seemed to be working together for a common good. She was also supremely glad that only the Cathari seemed to be present in the system. Other civilizations might interfere with the objectives of the Cathari Alliance and it was vital this section of the galaxy be united. Even though there was no real threat known to the Cathari Alliance at that time, it was still pragmatic to bring everyone into the galactic fold.

Her thoughts were brought back to the present by an indicator on her comm panel. First Dictator Zig was sufficiently recovered and wanted to resume his discussion. Liuna made the necessary arrangements and prepared herself mentally for the task. She hoped the human was ready as well. She didn't know what to expect but her long association with the humans taught her they were resourceful and always had a plan. She hoped she wasn't making a mistake.

After Liuna and Kwiu Zig had been evacuated from the wrecked atrium, Gallagher found himself talking to some smug Cathari security chief about just what prompted him to tackle the leaders and how he decided danger was imminent. Gallagher explained numerous times and answered the same question at least five different ways.

"Look, I saw a puff of smoke near an entryway to the atrium," Gallagher explained for the sixth time. "I thought it might be some kind of weapon being fired. I reacted. I'm damn glad I did too."

The Cathari nodded and kept going. "Is it normal for humans to accost planetary leaders like that?"

Gallagher snorted. If this guy only realized what humans did for *fun!* "Ever seen a football game?" When the Cathari just stared at him, he chuckled. "No, of course not. I acted because my training told me something bad was about to happen."

Gallagher trained at the Imperial War Academy here on Cathar Prime. He also previously trained with various military forces back on Earth. The Cathari officer seemed to finally be okay with his responses and led the way to a well furnished room.

"You can stay here. I'm sure someone will come collect you shortly." With that, the alien departed, leaving Gallagher alone, again.

"Hey this time I don't feel like a prisoner,"

Gallagher thought as he looked around the spacious quarters. Unlike aboard the D'lai ship, this room was more suited to his taste. Inside were comfortable chairs, a nice big and presumably soft bed, and various other amenities.

Gallagher searched the room and found the communications system. His last report to Earth had been made before he made that space walk to repair the solar panels. He accessed the comm panel and took a few minutes to familiarize himself with the icons. His time on Cathar Prime while in the Academy helped him to be able to understand the Cathari language and system of writing. Unlike on board the D'lai ship where he'd never seen or heard them before, here he was very familiar and it took him only a short time to find what he was looking for. He understood he wouldn't just initiate communication with Earth without the Cathari eavesdropping on him. He was fortunate he'd never been searched and still had in a hidden inner pocket a small device that enabled him to encrypt any communications. He pulled the device out and got to work contacting his superiors on Earth.

Voice communications were far more risky than text, so he opted to type out a brief synopsis of what happened in the last few days including his contact with the D'lai, the attack on Cathar Prime, and his present whereabouts. After he sent the brief message, he looked around the room to further familiarize himself with it.

Gallagher liked that the Cathari were supremely hospitable and they would go out of their way to make him comfortable while he was here. This room was no exception. He was familiar with Cathari cuisine but he was quite happy to find Earth delicacies as well. He grabbed some food and reclined on a very comfortable sofa while he ate. He started humming to himself the same tune stuck in his head outside *The Avenger* and that annoyed him.

"Why do they have to make those stupid ads so memorable?"

He also didn't expect a response from Earth any time soon. Earth was a dozen light years away and even the fastest communications array would mean it would take over an hour for the message to be received. Gallagher decided his stomach was full and he had nothing else to do to but doze off for a bit. He hadn't found much opportunity to rest since he had been captured. He also didn't have the energy to move from this sofa so he just rested his head on a nearby cushion and fell into a light but relaxing sleep.

HUMANS LOVED THEIR BUREAUCRACY. THEY WERE good at building layer upon layer of red tape and protocols. They loved it so much in fact it would often take days just to requisition a new work station.

The communique from Major Gallagher, however, was received like a bomb went off. His superiors reacted with shock and confusion. Earth's leaders learned about the D'lai from their frequent interactions with the Gathung. Their existence was one of the driving forces behind development of the cloaking technology. Earth's reciprocation with the Gathung taught it to be wary of other alien civilizations and to plan for inevitable altercations and possible interstellar war.

The message from Cathar Prime made its way to General Cai with striking rapidity. After he read the message, he realized he needed to alert the Secretary General. First, however, he needed to make sure the prototype was secure.

Earlier plans were made for deploying the planetary prototype secretly on one of Jupiter's moons and orders had been relayed to bring *The Avenger* in system. Earth had no colonies or ships in that region and they hoped by cloaking their ship en route to Jupiter, any observing aliens would not realize what was happening.

General Cai initiated contact with his Gathung counterpart.

"General," said the Gathung, "what now?"

General Cai bristled before replying, "when can we expect *The Avenger* to be in Sol System?"

The Gathung checked a screen and replied, "they are underway. Expect them within three hours."

Cai understood Gathung ships were much faster than Earth space craft and for once he was happy about that. The speed difference was a source of slight mistrust between the two worlds as the Gathung didn't seem terribly keen on sharing their propulsion methods.

Cai thanked the Gathung commander and clicked off. He needed a few minutes to gather some more intel and then he would be ready to talk with the Secretary General. He busied himself at his desk for a brief time and when he felt he was ready, he activated his comm panel to raise communications with Secretary General Allen.

After a few heartbeats, her face appeared on his screen.

"General. Report."

"Ma'am, *The Avenger* will be in system and en route to Jupiter within the next few hours. At that time we will deploy the prototype around Ganymede."

The Secretary General frowned, "I've received reports Major Gallagher is no longer aboard *The Avenger*. Can this test happen without him?"

Gallagher was the primary engineer working with the Gathung on the planet cloaking technology. His superior, Corey Hodges, was trained on the technology but had not done any of the day to day grunt work.

"Ma'am, we don't have many options. Hodges can run the test."

The Secretary General considered this for a long moment. "Make sure it works, General. We don't want to attract unnecessary attention."

"Yes, Ma'am," Cai said as he ended communications. He folded his hands in a gesture of good luck and waited.

GALLAGHER WAS AWAKENED FROM A DEEP SLEEP by a steady chiming sound coming from somewhere in the room. Startled awake, he was surprised to see the sun had set and a cool breeze was drifting in from an exterior window. He located the source of the noise and after a second or two figured out how to silence it. It was an incoming message from Ambassador Liuna. His presence was required. The message indicated an escort would be arriving shortly to bring him to the meeting location.

He took a few minutes and splashed some water on his face. He discovered in the mirror he could use a shave, but he suspected he didn't have the requisite time or perhaps even the necessary supplies. He decided the Cathari could wait and after rifling through some drawers in the equivalent of a bathroom, he was pleased to find all the amenities he would expect. He activated the sonic razor and efficiently removed his two day old stubble.

He just finished tidying up when another chime interrupted and he figured this one must be a doorbell or something similar. Unlike when he was on the D'lai ship, here he could open the door. The same security personnel who brought him to his quarters were standing outside. Wordlessly, they indicated he should follow. Gallagher shrugged and joined them. After a few minutes strolling through the peaceful passageways and voluminous open air rooms, he spied the Ambassador and the First Dictator reclining on a pair of sofas in a far corner of the atrium. Gallagher approached them..

When he was within earshot, he heard the Ambassador say "...disgruntled separatists targeted us when..." Liuna stopped when she saw the human approach.

"Thank you once again for joining us Gallagher," said the Ambassador. "I hope you had time to refresh yourself."

Gallagher nodded and pretended he hadn't heard anything. He made a mental note to include the bit of information in his next report to Earth. He settled down on a cozy seat and smiled at the First Dictator who did not return his smile. He grunted instead. Gallagher noted the sweat on the First Dictator's dark skin and the slight tremble but ignored it.

"Something else to report," he thought. He turned his attention to the two planetary leaders.

"Before the attack, we were talking about why you

were on my planet," said Liuna. She waited and Gallagher presumed this meant it was his turn to speak. His long association with the Cathari while he was in the Imperial Academy told him that while they were friendly, they were also no-nonsense in their approach. Gallagher relayed the experiences of the past few days. He paid particular attention to the events on the D'lai vessel. Even though the three humanoids were as different as they were alike, he recognized the looks that passed between the two leaders.

"You are a crewman on *The Avenger*," asked Kwiu Zig. Gallagher nodded. "My people tell me you are the primary engineer working on...," he hesitated before continuing, "the planetary cloak."

Ambassador Liuna let out an involuntary hiss of annoyance at this question. The First Dictator filled her in on the secret plans made between Gathung'l and Earth. She was not pleased by the admission but part of her understood. The Gathung were still reeling from the occupation and Earth was a willing collaborator. She doubted any other world in the Alliance would be so accommodating.

"Yes," Gallagher replied.

The two leaders began discussing the implications

while Gallagher listened. He already guessed the cloaking tech was a surprise to the Cathari, and he knew they would not approve. To his surprise, Liuna looked back at him.

"We need to get you back to your home. Events are moving along and there may be need of that tech. Soon."

He was inwardly pleased. While he didn't mind traveling on *The Avenger*, he really preferred to be back in his home system. First Dictator Zig worked his pad for a few very long seconds and then looked back up.

"*The Naomor* will bring Gallagher home."

Liuna sounded worried as she replied, "are you sure? We could just send him home with any number of merchant vessels."

Zig would broach no other method of travel. "No. My people know more about this tech than yours. He can work on deployment plans as we travel."

Liuna looked at Zig, startled. "You plan to be on board during the test?"

Zig smiled in the most hideous expression Gallagher had seen yet on a Gathung face. He didn't reply but his body language said everything.

Liuna waved them both away tiredly and her

aides assisted her out of the room. Kwiu Zig looked at Gallagher and together they left as well.

"Well," thought Gallagher, "I'm going home."

THE NAOMOR WAS HE FASTEST SPACE FARING vessel in the entire Gathung fleet. While it took *The Avenger* just over three hours to travel the twelve light years between the Gathung and Sol Systems, it took *The Naomor* a little less than two hours to travel a similar distance.

Gallagher was familiar enough with Gathung design to recognize the basic layout of this new ship. He spent the couple hours of the journey reading logs and revising checklists that would be required to initiate the planetary cloak. Engineers aboard *The Naomor* filled him in on the plans that had been hastily developed on Earth to deploy the prototype around the moon of Ganymede. Together they made sure *The Avenger* and the crew were ready for the test. It was apparent this deployment had to go off without a hitch. Gallagher didn't know all the details of the building tension, but he knew enough to understand this could be quite literally life and death for both their planets and perhaps even Cathar Prime itself.

*The Naomor* arrived near Jupiter and hailed *The Avenger*. Communications were risky with the D'lai lurking about somewhere in the solar system, but it was essential the commanders of the two ships communicated and they had to get Gallagher from one place to another. He really didn't want to get back into a small pod, but there was no other way. Beaming someone around with light waves or whatever was science fiction from Earth's early days of television, so even though Gallagher wished it was that simple, he understood it was not.

Arriving back on *The Avenger*, he was greeted by First Engineer Hodges.

"Man I thought you were frozen in space somewhere buddy," Hodges said as he embraced his fellow human.

"Naw, just jostled around a bit here and there," replied Gallagher, returning the embrace. "It's good to be back in familiar surroundings!"

The two engineers earnestly got to work on the prototype. The plan was to bring *The Avenger* within a hundred kilometers above Ganymede in stationary orbit. Once in place, they would launch the prototype. The ship had to be at least a thousand meters away from the device otherwise it risked being damaged. Once the prototype was deployed, a remote control station on the ship would be used to activate the tech. If successful, the planetary cloak would surround the moon with a force field that would imitate the cloak used on a space ship. The moon wouldn't really disappear, but the energy waves created by the prototype would "wrap" the surrounding star field around the planet, masking it.

The cloak would not fool anyone who was within visual range of a kilometer or less from the field. However, it would work to prevent the moon from being detected by any sensors and outside visual range, the moon would be invisible to the naked eye. The cloak had one other trick up its sleeve. No computer targeting would be possible. Modern targeting systems depended on sensor data and if there *was* no sensor data, then there could be no targeting. The deployed cloak could protect a planet or moon. It wasn't fool proof, but it most definitely could confuse a hostile threat.

After final checks were made by the team of engineers and the prototype was secured in the launch bay of *The Avenger*, Hodges and Gallagher gave the final go no go and the bay was depressurized. The bulky bay doors opened and the prototype used its built-in thrusters to maneuver out of the ship and into place. Everything was going well. Twenty minutes later the position of the prototype was confirmed, and holding his breath, Gallagher activated the cloak.

The bridge crew cheered loudly when Navigator Erth declared, "Sir, the moon has disappeared from sensors." Communications were instantly sent to the leaders of Earth and Gathung with news of a successful test. Orders were received to end the trial, bring the device back on board, and travel to the Saturn space port. Gallagher and Hodges sighed in relief when the prototype was safely stored back in the launch bay. They both beamed proudly at the successful launch but there was much work to be done. They needed to debrief and review the logs and data gathered. Gallagher also wanted to manually inspect the cloak for visible damage and make sure it could be deployed again if it became necessary to do so.

The men went their separate ways and got down to work.

Deep in space, the D'lai had detected a change in planetary objects from the neighborhood of Jupiter, but they could not determine what exactly their sensors had picked up. The data was relegated by an automatic process to a storage node for later evaluation. No D'lai had seen it. The deployment had gone off almost without a hitch.

# PART 2

## PART II - A HOSTILE GALAXY

## CHAPTER 6

As a young man, Kwiu Zig delighted in the evenings and the peace they brought. Most days he spent his time studying philosophy, the arts, mathematics and linguistics at Naomor University. He was a gregarious student and was always surrounded with friends and acquaintances. His mastery of his chosen fields of study meant those less able students always wanted to hang out with him. Kwiu didn't mind. He liked the company of his fellow Gathung.

Life on the planet was peaceful. The Gathung long ago left behind some of their more violent ways and achieved for the first time a delicate planetary balance between the two major continents. Kwiu was aware of the struggles of the Gathung on Sumor, but life was so comfortable he chose not to think of it. That was the attitude of most Gathung.

One morning Kwiu enjoyed a pleasant conversation with a young My named Shana. She was about his age, behind him one year in school, lovely, friendly, and most of all, she was *very* interested in Kwiu. His parents were adamant he should focus on his studies and avoid the pleasures of female company until he found a suitable placement in the Gathung hierarchy. Both his father and mother were highly placed scientists working on developing more efficient and cost effective chemical propulsion methods for the planets swiftly growing space program.

Kwiu understood all about his parents wishes, but he also really liked Shana. Like Kwiu, she came from a good home with a suitable family and they were well enough financially to not be a burden on a future spouse. Shana and Kwiu were finishing up a bowl of fruit they were sharing when a small tremor shook the ground. The Naomor continent was not immune to tremors, but they were far more common in Sumor. Nevertheless, Kwiu and Shana made sure they were safe and as soon as the tremor subsided, they laughed and returned to their pleasantries.

The sound of shouts and running feet caused Kwiu to look around himself. All around the young lovers, every Gathung around him was running out of buildings, their comm devices raised to ears or pressed close to faces. Kwiu and Shana laughed as the tremor hadn't been *that* bad to warrant such a reaction. They were just about to move to a quieter location when Shana's comm device began vibrating insistently. She smiled as she lifted the device up and then froze. One hand went to her throat and the other hand grabbed Kwiu. Thinking she was being playful, he laughed and turned to face her and stopped dead in his tracks. Her face displayed sheer terror. Kwiu picked up his own comm device and began to frantically read the reports that were coming across the web. That was when he also just happened to look *skyward*.

High overhead, dozens of enormous space ships settled into a high orbit over the planet Gathung'l. The vessels were spaced out evenly enough that from every vantage point on the planet's surface, a ship would be seen hovering high above. The Gathung had not yet developed space based defenses and only had geostationary satellites for such functions as weather and communications. The planet was unprepared for a large scale alien invasion, and the D'lai understood that. They always sought out easy to conquer planets in their growing quest for galactic domination. Gathung'l just happened to be on the list and their time had come.

Gathung'l had a weak planetary government and the inept leader of the planet quickly and without much cause surrendered his entire planet to the invaders. Not a single shot was fired from either side. On board the command ship of the D'lai fleet, newly installed Negotiator Ret D'iash smiled from her place on the bridge. They had long studied the planet and though they had a war like and violent past, they became pacifists as time elapsed and the D'lai understood conquering and occupying Gathung'l would be simple. Funnily enough, the Negotiator hadn't expected it to be quite as simple as taking a toy from a child, but it had been. Hundreds of thousands of *sdawij* clad D'lai descended to the surface and occupied major power plants, civic centers, schools, and thousands of other civic and government buildings around the planet.

Almost immediately, all civil liberties the Gathung and in particular the Naomorians enjoyed were suspended and martial law was instituted planet wide. Negotiator D'iash made a ceremonial show of entering the planetary capital and occupying the covered throne which the *former* leader of Gathung until very recently occupied. Any planetary inhabitants who resisted were executed on the spot in the most brutal method available. Just under a million Gathung citizens died horribly in the first week. The D'lai did not believe in providing an easy death to its enemies.

Kwiu and his family were shipped off to a work camp. His family had been identified by the D'lai occupiers as being relevant to the occupation's objectives. However, to make sure they cooperated, the D'lai viciously severed the lower legs of both his parents. If they couldn't run, they had no choice but to obey. Kwiu only escaped a similar fate because the D'lai also intended to press into service any young Gathung capable of being brainwashed and trained to serve the D'lai Authority. Kwiu never saw Shana again. Her family had been executed in one of the early purges of Gathung society and Kwiu didn't know if she was also dead or if she somehow escaped. Her memory was more of a torture for him than being imprisoned ever would be.

MANY YEARS AFTER THE D'LAI INVADED AND began occupying Gathung'l, Kwiu Zig was heading up an underground resistance movement aimed at disrupting as much of the D'lai plans as possible. He realized he didn't have the manpower or the technological skills to supplant the D'lai, but he sure had fun ruining as much of their strategies as he could.

"Kwiu, take a breath," exclaimed his father one evening. The family had been released from the work camp two years earlier after Kwiu's mother successfully developed cloaking technology for the D'lai. As a reward, Negotiator D'iash allowed the Zig family to move into comfortable quarters near the planet's capital city. The discovery of cloaking technology was a tremendous boon for the D'lai war effort and her people could show generosity when it was warranted.

Kwiu, however, refused to back down. His parents accepted his associations with a much rougher group of Gathung men than they would have during his University days. Kwiu took tremendous pains to keep his activities away from anything or anyone that could impact his family. They'd suffered enough at the hands of the D'lai Authority.

"I can't, tomorrow we are bombing a military

parade," huffed Kwiu to his father. "It may be the last chance we get while the Negotiator is on planet."

Kwiu's father shook his head and hushed his son. "Not here."

Negotiator D'iash was being recalled to the D'lai home world and being replaced by another Negotiator. Kwiu feared the new planetary leader would be just as bad as the old one and he wanted to send her off with a bang. Literally.

Kwiu's mother entered the room. She had been given prosthetic legs when she discovered the cloak and so as she stood in the small quarters her family had been given, she towered over Kwiu's legless father. After serving her husband his dinner, she took Kwiu aside.

The Gathung language had been banned along with most relics of Gathung society. Entire generations were now being raised who never spoke the native tongue. Kwiu spoke quietly with his mother in Gathungi, knowing what they said would probably not be understood even if it was by chance overheard.

"Kwiu, listen to me," his mother began. "You must be careful. You have a wondrous future ahead of you..."

"If only the blasted D'lai would leave us alone."

"Hush son and listen," his mother continued. "Do what you must, but prepare yourself," she said. Kwiu listened as any good son does and promised to himself whatever happened, he would make his parents proud.

He barely slept at all that night as he ran over plans and contingencies in his head. He awoke the next morning to a sound he had not heard in many, many years. The roar of cheers. He jumped out of bed and ran to the small living area where his parents were watching the vid screen in disbelief. Overnight, the D'lai seem to have just vanished from the face of the planet. The dozens of starships in orbit, the booted and covered soldiers, even the palace servants all seemed to be gone.

Kwiu could not believe it. He automatically assumed this was some cruel trick on the part of the D'lai. He kissed his parents and hurriedly left to meet up with his lieutenants. As word spread of more and more signs of a complete disappearing act, Kwiu acted swiftly. His men took control of the capital city using the same weaponry they planned to use on the military parade and a future unplanned event. With amazing rapidity, more and more Gathung flocked to his ranks and within a fortnight, Kwiu was nominally in command of the entire Naomor continent. Sumor soon followed.

ALL ALONE IN A LONELY PART OF SPACE, EARTH floats around a main sequence yellow star midway thought its life cycle. Part of a planetary system of eight planets and countless other dwarf planets, comets, asteroids, and moons, humans are the only sentient life that can be found anywhere within a dozen light years. Or so the humans thought as they were unaware of the dozens of alien civilizations in the Orion Arm alone.

Humanity managed to send probes into interstellar space and had begun colonizing the planet Mars and the moon of Titan. Of the almost eleven billion humans, less than a fraction of one percent lived off world. The main problem facing Earth was war and the resulting famine and disruption war brought. Feeding the billions of humans was a task in and of itself. The rich economies of the Western world competed for dominance with the more impoverished Eastern and third world nations. This conflict inevitably developed into three planet wide wars. The first two occurred less than thirty years apart. The third and by far much more devastating World War occurred midway through the following century.

After a turbulent era, the United States of America essentially collapsed into bickering factions leaving power vacuums that were filled by the more eager countries like China and Russia. After Russia invaded the newly discovered oil rich Mongolia, China retaliated by launching a small scale nuclear attack on Russian Crimea. This set off a chain reaction that escalated and engulfed almost every nation on the planet. When the United States refused to intervene on either the behalf of the Chinese or the Russians, the two sides executed a two pronged attack on America. The West Coast of the United States was overrun by the Chinese and Russia took advantage of that chaos and invaded Alaska and moved troops through neutral Canada and occupied the American Midwestern cities along the Great Lakes.

The US President, a scion of Trump era politics, sensed an opportunity and launched a full scale nuclear attack on the Arab nations of Syria and Iran. When the dust settled and the three major warring powers came to the table, one third of the planet was either a nuclear wasteland, or so devastated by war and famine that it might as well have been.

All the worlds economic powers met for a peace conference in Geneva, Switzerland three months after hostilities first erupted. European nations came together and demanded an end to the fighting. After the governments all met and eked out a very tentative and uneasy peace, a sense of calm seemed to pervade the planet and it was hoped that humans had begun to learn their lesson and work together for a change.

Then the Cathari arrived in orbit. Unlike the experience the Gathung endured when the D'lai suddenly appeared, the peaceful Cathari meant to aid the wounded planet and help nurse her back to health. Humans, however, didn't see their arrival as auspicious or friendly. As humanity is prone to do when disaster strikes, they panicked. The whole planet erupted into chaos, rioting, looting and mass casualties. Entire governments collapsed amidst the strife.

The Cathari were horrified, and not understanding the cause of the turmoil, they vanished from the skies. Calmer heads began to prevail and the governments that just signed a peace accord once again met in Geneva. This time the goal wasn't an end to fighting. The goal was to figure out what happened and prepare for it to happen again. Earth finally answered the age-old question of "are we alone?"

The answer was a resounding no.

AFTER THE CATHARI WITHDREW, THE CHAOS that erupted on Earth subsided slowly. After a time, the inhabitants realized that the danger seemed to have passed and calmer heads prevailed. World leaders gathered for an unprecedented summit with one overriding goal – protect the Earth. The leaders realized, however, that to protect the planet, they needed to put aside their international squabbling. Protecting Earth piecemeal wouldn't guarantee success.

One particular moment in the summit solidified the world powers. The leader of the famine ravaged country of Ghana approached the dais to address the assembled leaders. His nation had been hard hit not by the fighting or nuclear contamination, but by a simple lack of food. International shipping halted along with most aid and relief efforts. As the elderly leader began speaking, the room fell silent.

"Fellow leaders. I rise today because my country is dying. It is dying not because of what *we* have done. It is dying because of what *you* have done. You have ravaged the planet with your fights over oil and land. You have killed millions in your quest for domination.

You have Ghanaian blood on *your* hands. These aliens who have shown themselves in the skies are not the biggest threat to Ghana. You are the biggest threat. If we cannot unite then we must lay down and die."

With that, the Ghanaian leader withdrew. There was no applause, no cheers. The room was filled with almost every world leader on the planet, and not a single one of them could say a word. It was at this time that the British Prime Minister began circulating a half-baked plan that developed into a full-fledged blueprint for uniting the countries of Earth under the already established United Nations. Within ten days, every member country ratified the plan. On April 1, 2063, in a resolution passed unanimously by the United Nations General Assembly, Earth unified its disparate governments and for the first time in human history, humanity was united.

Global celebrations erupted around the planet. The United Nations moved to pass new rules and regulations that would help end global warming, send aid to nations in desperate need, and work toward cleaning up areas of the planet now polluted with nuclear waste. The planet also began earnestly looking toward the stars and working on its abilities to not only defend itself, but also to just "get out there" and see what else they could find. Private industry, which primarily took over the space race, launched its first human colonists to Mars. Plans were also made to colonize Titan. Those days of post-unification were exciting and humanity was filled with hope and a new ardor to get things done. That didn't mean the inherent skepticism and xenophobia died down. The planet was terrified of a full scale alien invasion. The overriding message that world leaders continued to pump out was simple: prepare, prepare, prepare.

Seven years after unification, the Cathari returned. This time, Earth was a little more ready for them.

UNLIKE THE GATHUNG AND HUMANITY, THE Cathari learned early in their civilization that they were not alone. Their star was born in a crowded area of the Orion Arm where multiple alien civilizations sprang up only a few light years distant from Cathar Prime. Cathari scientists discovered radio waves emanating from at least two distinct stellar neighbors around the same time that the planet was developing green technologies to wean itself off fossil fuels and other elements harmful to the planetary ecology.

Cathar Prime was also the only planet capable of sustaining life in its own solar system and so the reach for the stars developed much easier than it had for either Gathung'l or Earth. Both of those systems had wide-ranging planetary neighborhoods from which to explore and discover. The Cathari easily discovered the technology to travel between the stars. Their first foray into interstellar space took nearly fifty years but yielded amazing benefits and discoveries of life aboard space going craft. While that first voyage was still on its way to the nearest star which also happened to contain another alien race called the Scree, Cathari scientists worked feverishly to improve their technology.

Around the same time the Cathari arrived in Scree space, they were testing the first gravity FTL drives that would make the journey in months instead of years. It seemed improbable to the crew aboard the first deep space voyage that just as they arrived, another Cathari ship also entered the system. This was the beginning of the Cathari reaching out further into deep space. Within a decade, they traveled to seven other systems and encountered three other sentient civilizations.

None of the other civilizations were as advanced as the Cathari. A peace loving society, the Cathari shared their technology with these other planets and within fifteen years of their first contact with the Scree, the Cathari Alliance was born.

Those first days of the Alliance were heady and exciting for not only the Cathari but also for the other alien civilizations. Within the first twenty years, the Alliance grew to encompass seventeen other systems as far away as thirty light years from Cathar Prime. The Alliance grew and matured and in time, they developed objectives that would be mutually agreed upon regarding just how a new planetary system was greeted and welcomed into the wider galactic community. The Cathari met the Gathung seventy years before they also found Earth, and while their experience with Earth was unique among all their contacts, it did not deter them.

Three years after the Cathari withdrew from Earth and waited for the planet to grow up a little more, the Cathari encountered the D'lai. These Cathari had no idea of how their own civilization and the D'lai were intertwined in the distant past. A small fleet of twenty Cathari and Scree ships were traveling through a remote sector of the Orion Arm when they came upon an enormous fleet of one hundred D'lai ships. While the Cathari and their allies were peaceful explorers, the D'lai were conquerors. This fleet was en route to a fragile world in a nearby star system when the Cathari first met them.

Believing the motives of the D'lai to be pure, and disregarding any worry about the sheer size of the fleet as not relevant, a Scree commander initiated contact with the hostile D'lai. The Scree were even more naive than the Cathari and didn't understand the concept of violence in any form. One D'lai battleship broke from the ranks of the larger fleet and attacked the innocent Scree ship that failed to remain in tight formation with the rest of the small exploration fleet, destroying it and ending the lives of seventy-five Scree crewmen. The Cathari, misunderstanding the attack, attempted to broker a peace with the D'lai fleet. The fleet turned its planet conquering weapons on the Cathari and remaining Scree vessels and within minutes, the twenty ships of the fleet were dead in space. A reconnaissance mission sent by Cathar Prime when their fleet didn't arrive at its designated coordinates discovered the destroyed ships. An investigation of what happened revealed the existence of the D'lai Authority. Senior leadership on Cathar Prime hid the truth of the battle from their allies in an attempt to assuage their own guilty past.

Cathar Prime, it's alliance, and most notably the Scree, barely recovered. In time, the Alliance objectives were further refined and they took baby steps once more in their galactic exploration. A deadly lesson had been learned, and it would never be forgotten.

Ret D'iash was tired. She sat in her office in the capital of Gathung'l going over endless paperwork. This was her first posting as a Negotiator and of all the planets the D'lai conquered in her service to the D'lai Authority, this planet was much more than a challenge. It was a nightmare. While the Gathung as a whole mostly surrendered to the more technologically advanced and militarily superior D'lai, there was an active resistance that kept her security forces very occupied.

Several weeks earlier, Negotiator D'iash received revised orders that would station her on board *The*

*Spector*, a battleship that the D'lai Authority intended to use as part of its buildup to the final conquering of the Cathari. In truth, the D'lai had been planning on conquering Cathar Prime for decades. D'iash wasn't sure if the plan would ever come to fruition but she was nothing if not loyal to the Authority.

The D'lai Authority had a military heavy command structure. The few civilians in leadership were all placed there owing to *who* they knew as opposed to *what* they knew. The titular head of the Gathung Occupation Command was a smug D'lai civilian who was always challenging the real authority. He also was an apologist and always tried to take the side of the conquered over the conquerors.

"Negotiator, I *insist* that we invite the former royal family to the hand off."

"That is not going to happen," said D'iash. "In the first place, most of that family is dead. In the second, we don't invite *former* planetary leaders to do anything, least of all participate in handover ceremonies!"

"Ret...," he began. D'iash's eyes flashed a warning, "Negotiator, this is just the thing that might foster good will!"

"Foster good *will*?" D'iash grabbed her pad and

showed it to him. "Like these terrorists killing our security forces? *That* good will?"

"Negotiator..."

"Further more, if I *wanted* your advice I would have summoned you. I am the real authority on this planet!"

"For 12 more hours, *Negotiator*."

He stormed out of her office and D'iash shook her head. It was hard enough to keep these ordinary Gathung in line but to have one of her own race challenging her was more than she was willing to deal with.

Many years earlier on D'lai, it had been drilled into her that military officers lead and civilians plead. That was a lesson that she was not going to forget, even if she was being transferred off planet. She ruled Gathung with an iron fist for almost a century and she was not about to bow to them now.

Negotiator D'iash, however, was worried. She didn't worry about Gathung'l. She fretted over her own people. The changeover in planetary command was supposed to go off smoothly and the intention was to allow the Negotiator to focus on other areas of the D'lai Authority. Mere hours before the handover was to formally occur, D'iash received hurried orders from the D'lai home world. All D'lai missions were being canceled and every Negotiator and the fleets at their disposals were to return to evacuate the planet claimed by the D'lai as their home. Scientists determined that the local sun was about to go supernova and time was of the essence in salvaging as much of the D'lai civilization as possible.

D'iash did not have time to consider the implications. She sprang into immediate action and with a few swift taps on the keyboard she issued an emergency planetary evacuation. The next six hours were controlled chaos as every D'lai on the planet jumped on transport ships. The Negotiator's staff destroyed as many digital records as they could to prevent them from falling into Gathung hands.

Every D'lai on Gathung'l was lifted into orbit and the fleet was ready to depart. D'iash took one last look at Gathung'l and gave the order to engage the FTL drives. The seventy light year journey would take a week to complete. The urgency with which the D'lai Authority recalled her fleet was a serious cause for concern. She had no idea what to expect when she arrived home.

The next weeks were going to be the most challenging of her life. Once that star exploded, the D'lai would never be the same. Deep inside, Negotiator Ret D'iash was excited for the implications. This could be her chance and she was going to take it no matter what the cost.

The D'lai home world is one of four planets orbiting a massive star seventy-five light years from Earth. The system is the same age as Sol but unlike Earth's star, which is midway through its lifespan, the D'lai sun was nearing the end. The D'lai claimed this planet and the star system a millennium ago and set out conquering other planets a thousand years before humans discovered electricity. The drive to build a civilization that rivaled every other was critical to the future of the D'lai people. Consequently, while not much attention was paid to Earth for most of its history, almost every space faring civilization was aware of the D'lai.

Hours after the fleet left the neighborhood of Gathung'l, Negotiator D'iash received communication from another nearby fleet. She collapsed into her chair, stunned, saddened, and more dangerous than ever before. During the journey home, the D'lai sun exploded. The resulting shock wave destroyed every planet, D'lai ship, moon, asteroid, and any other stellar objects within the ever growing blast radius.

Billions of ordinary D'lai were incinerated minutes after scientists detected a massive pulse of neutrinos from the local star. The supernova would over time grow to affect any world within twenty light years.

The result of the destruction only emboldened the now homeless D'lai fleets. Under the direction of D'iash, a thousand ships from all over the Orion Arm of the galaxy rendezvoused in an empty star system ten light years from D'lai. Consisting of over one hundred full fleets, each fleet with its own Negotiator, the remaining D'lai coalesced around an ambitious plan to find a new home for the second time in its history. This time the D'lai would not be destroyed by a single nova or the whim of their own ancestors who left them to die in the void of space. Their targets were outside the destruction zone of the still growing shock wave and would not be sterilized with radiation. Each of the vast fleets were given separate directives with the ultimate goal of finally conquering each world. With any luck, within fifty years, the D'lai would rebuild their civilization and be ready to occupy Cathar Prime, Gathung'l, and the infant and still unaware Earth.

After Gathung'l had been liberated from the D'lai, Kwiu Zig declared himself the First Dictator of a United Gathung People. As a result of the occupation, the planet was covered with incredible advances in infrastructure that the Gathung on their own might never have achieved. The remains of D'lai technology that had not been scooped up on their hasty retreat now formed the basis of an ever expanding scientific boom. Vast rail systems, air and orbital flight, and resource conservation had been the unwitting gift of the D'lai.

As part of the handbook on occupation the D'lai seemed to use on all their conquered worlds, they employed the populace in building and retrofitting each planet for their own purposes. Gathung'l was no exception. Leading scientists and thinkers were able to employ the discarded technology and the Gathung launched themselves into space to explore their solar neighborhood. Within two years, the Gathung were leaving their own systems and traveling among the stars. One Gathung trait the D'lai had not taken into much account was the incredible aptitude for engineering and the sciences that, on Gathung, was common.

Kwiu Zig used every available resource at his

considerable disposal to advance his civilization. The civilization voraciously explored and expanded their influence. Not only did the Gathung join the Cathari Alliance within fifteen years of their freedom from the occupation, they soon were indispensable to the Cathari who were able to slowly retreat from their own exploration and leave matters up to the Gathung. When the Cathari established loose diplomatic ties with Earth, the Gathung were right there as part of the negotiations. Without the knowledge of the titular Cathari leaders of the Alliance, Kwiu Zig through his intermediaries were making overtures of closer relations with Earth. He recognized a kindred spirit between Humanity and the Gathung.

The civilian leaders of Earth were not as enthusiastic of deeper ties with the Gathung, but the military was enthralled. These early discussions formed the basis of technology sharing between Gathung'l and Earth that would not have passed muster with the Cathari Alliance's peaceful objectives. This did not deter either planet. Earth, with the help of the Gathung, were able to develop faster than light travel much sooner than would be expected with the much slower pace of technology swaps envisioned by the Cathari. While the Cathari always allowed their technological advances to be shared, they meted out those advances incrementally to avoid letting a planet evolve too quickly. As a result of Gathung'l and their willingness to share everything with Earth, within a decade, regular expeditions were traveling between the two worlds and Earth was building the space hub near Saturn. Because the Gathung maintained the bureaucracy of the Cathari Alliance, the Cathari were unaware of the closer ties. They studiously scrubbed reports of increased human activity and sanitized logs. It became the big secret of the galaxy and if the Cathari had the forethought to look for it, they would have been horrified. Of course, they were also unaware of the growing D'lai threat. Conversely, the D'lai were most definitely aware of Earth's growing abilities and reveled in Cathar Prime's inattention.

Kwiu Zig marveled that such a technologically advanced species as the Cathari could be so naive about the rest of the galaxy. He thrilled at the prospect of using that naivete against them.

LIUNA WAS A MID LEVEL DIPLOMAT WHEN THE Cathari made its early stage diplomatic ties with

Earth. She had been among one of the first embassies established in London. She had never been on any planet other than Cathar Prime and so the differences between the two planets were striking. The increased gravity on Earth made her feel weak and it took weeks before she felt normal in her own skin. London was a crazy jumble of historical buildings, modern sky rises, air and ground vehicles and foot traffic. Her home on Cathar Prime was different. Where humans always seemed to be going *somewhere* Cathari seemed to always move about more calmly.

One of the first things she did on Earth was to explore some of the stunning architecture and palaces and castles that littered the city and surrounding countryside. She took in the thousand-year history of England and loved exploring the Victoria and Albert Museum when she had any free time at all. She traveled to as many regions of the planet as she could under the auspices of diplomacy but in reality it was to *be* where humans spent their entire known history. From the fjords of Norway to the Statue of Liberty, she imagined the life of ordinary humans as she worked hard to understand their cultural and yet bloody past. She was amused at the notions of fellow tourists she encountered when visiting the Giza

Plateau. Those humans who weren't scared of her loved to ask if her species had been responsible for the pyramids. She would try to explain how humans built these huge edifices all on their own, but it seemed that humans really wanted to believe aliens were responsible. If aliens built the pyramids, Liuna had never seen or heard of any similar constructions on any of the dozen worlds in the alliance.

The Cathari had no concept of absolute power or even constitutional authority and so one of the most thrilling experiences had been when the aged King of England, William IV, invited the entire Cathari delegation to what was called a garden party on the grounds of Buckingham Palace. The stuffy old gentleman and his family delighted in exposing the visiting alien diplomats to what they considered to be polite society. Even though she read all about their history, actually meeting people who valued titles over scientific advancement puzzled and awed her. However, Liuna perceived that as much as she enjoyed exploring Earth, it was critical that she also focus on building up the diplomatic ties. Her superiors felt she was spending too much time delving into history and not enough time collaborating with her human diplomatic colleagues. She argued unsuccessfully that comprehending the human condition was almost more important than working with them on the more mundane tasks of galactic diplomacy. She believed that it was critical to the long term success of any future alliance that they understand the soul of humans, otherwise they could be blindsided by aspects of their society that were contrary the missions objectives. She feared the Cathari had not learned the stinging lessons of their disastrous encounter with the D'lai many years ago.

Liuna redoubled her cultural and diplomatic efforts. She wrote extensive reports on the blending of culture and diplomacy and logged every experience she'd had while on the planet. Her hard work paid off when she was assigned as the cultural attache. This new post allowed her the freedom to expand her visits and historical studies of the planets history. She grieved over some of the darkest periods of human history – war, slavery, rampant violence, and disease. She worked in vain to compare their history with her own. There really was no comparison and she wondered aloud to anyone who would listen if Earth would have experienced those growing pains if she realized she was not alone in the universe – that Earth's existence *mattered.*

Liuna also feared that Earth would grow up too quickly. The long term objectives of the Cathari Alliance could be imperiled by the inquisitiveness of humans. She hoped she was wrong. Everything depended on Earth joining the Alliance and not going rogue.

CHAPTER 7

After the successful test of the prototype planetary cloak, *The Avenger* was ordered to deliver it to the Saturn space hub for further testing and duplication. Earth recently commissioned a research lab that was going to replicate the device and conduct final tests on it before it could be deployed. It had *originally* been planned to deploy on *Voyager* but that plan needed to be revised and an alternate ship was being sought out.

The Gathung did not know Earth planned on using the technology independently. While they held copies of all the blueprints and other essential components, they did not have a working prototype and expected that Earth would continue to work with them in manufacturing and development. First Dictator Zig had plans to mask his planet from the outside world with no intention of being unprepared if the D'lai decided to return to finish what they started.

On Earth, General Cai monitored the deployment and the delivery. He fretted over the loss of *Voyager*. Plans had been prepared to use the ship to carry out a full-scale deployment of the cloak. Cai didn't trust the Cathari or the Gathung and he had no usable intelligence on the D'lai.

Owing to the compartmentalized nature of military and civil government, he did not feel the need to brief Secretary General Allen on the most recent developments. His intention was to deploy the cloak in high Earth orbit so that at any time with very little notice, he could protect the planet, fulfilling what he saw as his mission.

"General," began an aide, "the cloak prototype has been delivered to our secure lab on Titan."

General Cai leaned back in his chair and relaxed.

"Very good Lieutenant. Hail the lab."

After a momentary delay, the reply came, "Sir I have the lab on comms."

"This is Titan Secure Lab Alpha, Captain Jiron reporting."

"Captain Jiron," said the General, "what is the status of the cloak prototype?"

"Sir, the prototype was delivered and is in a clean room undergoing inspection."

"Very good. Major Gallagher is at the hub and will take personal charge of the device."

"Sir?" Jiron was surprised. "We've not had sufficient time to copy it."

"You heard me Captain," said Cai, "Do what you can but time is of the essence. The Major will have further orders when he arrives."

"Yes, sir." Captain Jiron ended the transmission.

Cai stood and left his office. Some fresh air would do him good.

Upon arrival at Titan Secure Lab Alpha, Gallagher asked the desk sergeant for Captain Jiron. A few moments later, an older man wearing a white lab coat over his military uniform arrived. He shook hands with Gallagher.

"Major, good to meet you," said Jiron. "Can I get you anything? You must be tired from the trip."

"No Captain. Take me to the device."

The pair passed through several interior doors.

Gallagher noted the increasing level of security the deeper into the facility he went.

"Captain, I will need a secure comm as well."

Jiron nodded and led Gallagher to a small office. The room was bare except for a desk, a chair, and an ample window that overlooked the clean room where Gallagher could see the device. Technicians were moving around the device inspecting it with hand held instruments. He moved to the small desk and activated the comm. Entering a secure address on the computers keyboard, he waited.

After a delay, a menu appeared on the screen. Gallagher read through a short list of communications and found the one he was looking for.

[Begin Communication]

From: Space Operations – General Lin Cai

Transfer and secure prototype to *Atlantis*. Remain with prototype. *Atlantis* scheduled to depart for Earth orbit in 12 hours.

[End Communication]

Gallagher closed the message and after a few

minutes of reading through others, including one from his parents, he switched off the comm.

First Dictator Zig died of Zeisen syndrome six hours after delivering Major Gallagher to *The Avenger*. Zig had been sharing a meal with his top aides and started to slur his words. He recognized that something was not quite right and so with the help of a trusted assistant, Zig made his way to his quarters. He expected to rest and feel better after a few hours. Instead, as soon as he entered the room, a violent seizure struck him. His horrified aide tried to assist but having no medical knowledge only made matters worse. The First Dictator suffocated and was dead before anyone else could help him.

Officers and governmental officials on *The Naomor* were stunned by Zig's sudden death. They overcame a temporary paralysis of inaction and began preparing plans for not only a transition to new leadership but also how to tell the galaxy at large that Zig was dead. Protocol had been developed as Zig showed signs of advancing age. Immediately upon the First Dictator's death, the plans had been unsealed and transmitted to the appropriate individuals. As with everything they did, the Gathung leadership followed the plan with ruthless efficiency. The Gathung people would not be informed of the demise of their leader. Zig made special orders that his death would be kept secret as long as possible owing to what he believed was an impending re-emergence of the D'lai. He long suspected that the resulting chaos of his death would be the catalyst required for another planetary occupation.

Unfortunately for Kwiu Zig, the spies on his staff alerted the D'lai. The directives planned out by Negotiator D'iash and others in the D'lai Authority were enacted. Within six hours of the First Dictator's death, D'lai fleets in the Sol system, the Gathung System, and the Cathar system moved into a forward readiness position. The power vacuum on Gathung'l was a perfect opportunity for the D'lai and they would not fail to take advantage of it.

Negotiator D'iash was overjoyed with the news. The D'lai had been planning a three front invasion of the major galactic powers for decades. They initially planned on conquering the tiny world of Scree but the D'lai had a distaste of the weak planet and when Earth began growing in influence, plans were scrapped and Earth was added to its target list. Scree could be mopped up in auxiliary actions.

The death of the First Dictator was one of the final acts that were required for completion of the plans. After conferring with her top commanders via encoded communications in the three star systems, she was ready to put into place one of the last strategies required to ensure a smooth conquest. Her agents on Cathar Prime moved into place in Ambassador Liuna's palace. Similar behavior was occurring on Earth near the headquarters of the United Nations. D'iash presumed any new leader of the Gathung would be aboard his flagship and so she relayed orders to every ship in the Gathung system to be on the lookout for that ship. One part of the plan was to remove the planetary leaders. Zig's death was a helpful bonus. With luck, the leaders of Earth and Cathar Prime would be taken out. The resulting chaos would benefit the invasion plans.

The D'lai had been working to break the Gathung and Earth cloak technology and thanks to well-placed spies, they had the frequencies that would help them sniff out *The Naomor* as long as any appropriately configured sensors were within range of it. None of the ships near Earth were close enough so they would have to detect *The Naomor* sneaking into Gathung'l orbit.

Once all three of the massive fleets were in position, the order would be given to decapitate the remaining governments. Negotiator Ret D'iash smiled in satisfaction at the approaching success of her long planned revenge.

As soon as Major Gallagher safely secured the prototype cloak on *Atlantis,* the order was given and the ship left the Saturn space hub and set course for Earth. Gallagher stayed with the device in a small room off the launch hangar. He had no idea of the events unfolding elsewhere in the galaxy but he had his orders.

"Major, you don't have to sit here the entire voyage," said a crew member from the door of the office.

"I'm not going anywhere buddy," replied Gallagher.

The crew member shrugged and offered him some food. Gallagher politely declined. He busied himself with fine-tuning the deployment checklists he and Hodges worked on before and after the test deployment on Ganymede. Military preparedness would not allow him to leave anything to chance.

Several hours later, Gallagher stood to stretch and looked out a window as Earth came into clear view outside the craft. It had been months since he had seen his home planet. The blue planet was breathtaking from this vantage point.

Returning to his small desk, he logged into his comm panel and reported. He was surprised that as soon as he sent a status update, an incoming message flashed on the small screen. He opened the message.

"Major," said General Cai.

"General, I didn't expect..."

Cai cut him off. "We have received reports of odd behavior from the Gathung flagship. I don't know what is going on but I need that device, now."

Gallagher reflected for a moment. "Sir, I may have an idea."

Surprised, Cai waited. "Yes, Major?"

"Sir, while I was on Cathar Prime meeting with Ambassador Liuna and First Dictator Zig, I observed the First Dictator. He was not well," he said.

"What do you mean, not well?"

"Have you ever heard of Zeisen General?"

"Yes, an illness that affects..." The General stopped speaking and turned and spoke to a nearby aide in a low whisper. Turning back to the camera, he said, "Zig is ill, Major?"

"Sir, I can't know for sure. I'm not a doctor. During my time on Cathar Prime at the Academy, one of my Gathung teachers had Zeisen. I recognized the signs in the First Dictator."

General Cai turned to speak to the same aide. He turned back to the camera, his face flushed.

"That cloak needs to be ready to go now."

"Yes sir," said Gallagher. The message ended and Gallagher raced from the room to the bridge. A few moments later he pulled the Captain aside.

"Major, what is this?"

"Captain, I have orders to deploy. Your navigator has the coordinates. We need to get there."

The Captain looked uncertain.

"Right now, Captain."

The navigator was instructed to insert *Atlantis* into high Earth orbit. Gallagher left the bridge and ran down the corridors to the launch bay. He had been assigned override codes and entered them on an exterior control panel. Crew members ran from the area when the warning lights came on indicating the bay door was opening. Gallagher used the panel and remotely launched the cloak.

After the twenty-minute orbital insertion was complete, Gallagher ran some final tests. He then activated the panel's comm and informed General Cai of successful placement. A moment later he received the order to engage the cloak.

Everyone on board *Atlantis* and several other ships in Earth orbit stared in amazement as the cloak deployed. Within minutes the force field wrapped itself around the planet and Earth was no longer visible from space. Alarms went off on every orbital platform and vessel warning of the complete disappearance of the planet. On Earth, the sunlight seemed to dim slightly but there was no other obvious sign of any changes. Humans and aliens alike went about their normal business.

In London, Secretary General Allen was grabbed by her security agents while she was in a meeting with her ministers and rushed into a secure bunker below the building. General Cai was waiting for her.

"General, what is going on?"

"Ma'am, we have reason to believe that First Dictator Kwiu Zig is dead."

Allen gasped and collapsed into a seat.

"What? How?"

"Our agents believe the First Dictator suffered from a fatal disease. Odd behavior of the Gathung flagship indicated something was up."

"What odd behavior?"

"Ma'am, less than an hour ago, the First Dictator's ship cloaked itself."

"Why is that odd behavior? We all have..."

"Ma'am, his ship was in Earth orbit."

"And this agent..."

"Gallagher. He is the Major in charge of the planetary cloak. He was with Zig only days ago on Cathar Prime."

The General continued to brief the Secretary General. The room was filled with frenetic energy as aides and government ministers rushed in and out.

An aide approached the Secretary General. "Ma'am, orbital ships have indicated that Earth disappeared from sensors and visuals."

Allen turned toward the General. "Explain!"

"On my authority I have ordered the cloak activated. We don't know what is happening and it is my responsibility to this planet to keep it safe."

The same aide had a pained expression on his face. Allen motioned for him to continue.

"Ma'am, we also have captured two armed aliens near your office," the aide said.

"D'lai agents," asked the General.

"No, sir. They claimed to be D'lai and they were covered head to toe in this weird looking fabric..."

General Cai felt his stomach heave. He read the reports from Gallagher about his encounter after being captured by the D'lai.

"The D'lai!" The General was about to step to a command console when the aide stopped him.

"No, sir. These aliens...they are Cathari."

The room fell silent as the implication was understood.

"General, the D'lai and the Cathari..." she trailed off.

"Madam Secretary General, I believe that the D'lai *are* the Cathari. They are the same species."

At that moment, proximity alarms began blasting from every available speaker. The warning could only mean one thing. General Cai looked at his command console and froze.

"Ma'am, a fleet of at least... my God... a hundred ships just appeared in orbit of the moon."

The General scrolled through numerous pages on his console, then stood and cleared his throat.

"Ma'am, we recognize the ship configurations. They match the three ships we were tracking near Neptune."

"What does that mean General?"

"Ma'am, if our intel is correct... these ships are D'lai," said the General. "An invasion has begun."

From orbit, Gallagher swore when the enormous fleet showed up on the *Atlantis* sensors. Every ship that was capable cloaked. Everyone else began fleeing the planet.

The D'lai were here.

ON THE BRIDGE OF *THE NAOMOR*, THE INTERIM leader of the Gathung Bresu Xid read documents that were transmitted to him upon the death of the First Dictator. Kwiu Zig, knowing his end was near, prepared down to the last detail not only plans for his succession but also a detailed plan to slowly reveal the news of his death and how he was to be remembered. Zig handpicked his temporary successor and hoped he would be strong enough to assume full command of the far-flung Gathung people.

Immediately upon Zig's death, Xid implemented

the established protocol and ordered the ship to cloak and all communications to cease. An automatic lock was placed on any transmissions to Gathung'l and any other planet or ship. *The Naomor* prepared to depart Earth orbit and return home where the new leader would enact further protocols outlined by Zig to keep the citizens of his planet unaware that anything out of the ordinary happened. It was the express wish from the now dead leader that a swift transition take place and new leadership be installed to forestall any planetary chaos or to give allies and enemies a chance to take advantage of the situation.

"Leader Xid," said a tactical officer on the bridge.

Xid looked up from his pad. "Yes."

"Sir, sensors indicate that the planet Earth has disappeared entirely."

Xid recognized what happened. Earth engaged the cloaking device both planets worked for the past several years to perfect. He also realized he would be unable to hail the planet as any sensors and communications devices would not be able to penetrate the cloak. That was after all the entire intent of the cloak – to make the planet not only invisible but unreachable.

"Check for orbital ships. Find out..."

At the exact moment the warnings sounded on Earth, similar warnings erupted from the bridge of *The Naomor*. Xid searched for the reason and stood. On sensors, they detected the uncloaking D'lai armada.

"Navigation, disembark from Earth. Return to Gathung'l. Now!"

Crew members on the bridge enacted the orders as Xid considered next steps. Warily he sat down again and searched through his pad for information he sought. When he found the document he was looking for, he flung the pad across the deck of the bridge, cracking the device nearly in half causing several bridge officers to duck defensively.

An aide carefully approached the enraged Xid. "Sir?"

"We don't have our own copy of that cloak?"

The aide bowed and looked away. "No, *The Avenger...*"

Xid ordered a break in protocol and ordered his crew to contact *The Avenger*. He had to get a copy of that cloak. He could not believe that Earth would betray his people.

After a brief flurry of conversation, his aide said,

"Sir, there was only one copy... Earth has it. We do have technical specs..."

Interim Leader Xid left the bridge in fury. He'd only been in charge for a short time and he had absolutely no idea what to do next. He prayed Gathung'l was safe.

Thousands of kilometers from Gathung'l, another D'lai armada uncloaked and approached the planet. It would take *The Naomor* hours to reach home. The D'lai were much, much closer.

ON CATHAR PRIME, AMBASSADOR LIUNA reviewed disturbing reports from the Sol System. It appeared from all available data that Earth disappeared. To make matters worse, her colleague and friend Kwiu Zig's flagship had also vanished. She did not know why Earth was gone from all orbital sensors. Only a few days ago Kwiu Zig had been telling her of secret plans that had been implemented between Earth and Gathung'l, but he departed the planet with Major Gallagher before he provided clear details.

Liuna put down her tea and sighed. Galactic events were swirling so fast she hadn't had time to adapt and respond to them. A part of her longed for the days when she'd been a junior diplomat on Earth, enjoying the sights and sounds of a planet not yet come to terms with the full scale of what membership in the wider community of civilizations meant.

Her thoughts were interrupted by alerts blaring from her comm panel. She moved to silence them and her hand froze over the icon. She whirled to check another monitor that displayed sensor data for every world in the Cathari Alliance. Several aides ran into the office, each shouting, attempting to be understood. Liuna stared at the monitor as an enormous D'lai fleet appeared beyond the orbit of Cathar Prime. Another fleet emerged near Gathung'l and a third near Earth. A full scale invasion was underway. Liuna knew what this meant. The years of hiding the truth violently erupted in disaster. Cathari leadership kept secrets so devastating that only a few living among her people knew or even suspected the truth.

Acting swiftly, she ordered her aides to put the planet on alert. Just because the Cathari were peaceful did not mean they were not prepared for the eventuality of invasion. She just responded to an aide's query when a brilliant flash of light temporarily blinded everyone in the room. Seconds later a tremendous shock wave shook the building, shattering every window and knocking everyone in the room to the floor.

Regaining her composure Liuna rose and stared out the remains of her window. To her horror, an enormous fireball was rising in the near distance. Liuna braced herself and began a calming mantra she had been taught by her mother for times of distress. A wall of fire was approaching. Seconds later, the heat seared and then vaporized everything and everyone.

The blast that destroyed the Cathari capital was a direct result of orders from Negotiator Ret D'iash presently in orbit of Cathar Prime. She witnessed from an observation deck as the blast, visible from space, rose above the planet. She felt no remorse. Of all the civilizations in the galaxy, the one most hated and despised by the D'lai was the Cathari. Their smug peaceful exploration represented a level of naivete so galling that every D'lai child was taught to hate them from infancy.

The Cathari banished the ancestors of the D'lai a thousand years in the past, but the pain of that betrayal was still felt by every living D'lai. Their disdain was so inbred into the DNA of the D'lai that even a further ten thousand years would not dissipate it one tiny bit. To be banished from the paradise of Cathar Prime and damned to roam the galaxy in primitive ships searching for a new home was an injury too deep to ever heal.

The catalyst of a star gone nova and a civilization once more on the brink was all that the Negotiator needed to implement plans laid out by her predecessors in the distant past. It was finally time to destroy the Cathari and every single thing their Alliance stood for and accomplished.

As D'iash ordered her command ship to continue attacking the planet, she smiled. One more phase was now complete. The D'lai, ancient siblings of the Cathari, were coming home – to stay.

## CHAPTER 8

Captain Ziqna was roused from an unsatisfying sleep in his quarters by the insistent chiming of his comm panel. Grunting, he slapped open the channel.

"This better be good," he said.

"Captain, we have received unconfirmed reports *The Naomor* has gone silent and cloaked in orbit of the Earth."

Ziqna sat up and wiped his eyes to clear them. For a moment he wondered why he had been alerted to something so routine. After coming awake, it hit him.

"Something is wrong," he said to himself. He dressed in his uniform as fast as possible and departed from his quarters. He ran up the corridor and stormed on to the bridge.

"Report!"

The tactical officer on duty at this early hour cringed as he turned to face the Captain.

"Sir, all we know is that communications and cloak..."

"Yes, I got *that* when you woke me up!"

Ziqna sat in his command chair and thought for a moment. What he needed at this moment beside more intel was coffee. The humans on his ship introduced him to this particular drink and he soon discovered the stimulating properties. It didn't take him and others on the ship long to grow dependent on it. He turned to the tactical officer.

"If you can't give me useful intel, get me a damn cup of coffee."

The officer hurried from the bridge.

"Navigator, what is our current heading and status?"

Arvesp turned in her seat to face Ziqna.

"Sir, we are nearing the FTL insertion coordinates for travel back to Gathung'l."

The tactical officer returned with Ziqna's coffee.

"Hmm...hold position Navigator."

"Aye."

Ziqna was puzzled by the behavior of *The Naomor* but he feared something happened on board. He thought back to when he had last seen the First Dictator. He understood the First Dictator was suffering from Ziesen even if everyone tried to pretend otherwise. The Captain had an uncle who also was afflicted by the disease and so he understood the symptoms. Ziqna understood an elderly Gathung with the syndrome would be fine one moment and dead the next. It was not so much a progressive disease as it was unpredictable. With sudden clarity, Ziqna froze.

"My God...," said the Captain aloud without meaning to.

Everyone on the bridge turned to face him.

"Tactical! Cloak the ship!"

The tactical officer started to protest it was illegal to cloak inside a star system. He complied when the Captain gave him a look that might have killed him. Everyone on board remembered what he had done to Zika and no one wanted to become a corpsicle.

"Cloak is confirmed, Captain."

"Navigator, return to Earth at maximum speed."

"Aye Captain."

"Communications, monitor all channels but do not send any communications of our own!"

Once the ship was safe and headed back to Earth, the Captain opened a channel to address the entire crew.

"This is the Captain. I do not have proof of what I am about to say but if it is true, our lives and our mission will change in ways we cannot yet know." The Captain cleared his throat. "I believe First Dictator Kwiu Zig is dead or incapacitated," he paused for a moment before continuing, "there are protocols in place for a change in leadership and even though I have not received any official confirmation, I am enacting those protocols."

The Captain was about to continue when the tactical officer jumped from his station and shouted, "Captain!"

Captain Ziqna turned and he froze when he saw the look on his officers face.

"Captain, we've just detected an armada of D'lai ships."

"Location?"

"Sir, it is coming from... Earth."

"Do we continue our heading Captain?" Asked Arvesp Erth.

"We continue."

It would take *The Avenger* another hour to be close enough to Earth to gather any more information. Ziqna took time to reacquaint himself with the protocols for leadership changes and also what to do in case of a D'lai invasion. He was rather young when the D'lai left Gathung'l but his people had a long memory and they passed down as much of their knowledge as possible.

THE D'LAI FLEET IN ORBIT ABOVE CATHAR PRIME was over one hundred battleships strong. When the fleet arrived, the commanders received orders from Negotiator D'iash to proceed to battle readiness positions. On board the ships of the fleet were landing craft capable of deploying tens of thousands of D'lai troopers.

Each ship was capable of leveling gigantic sections of the planet from orbit using weapons developed over a millennium of hate filled D'lai single-mindedness. Similar to the effects of a nuclear blast, the D'lai planet killers delivered the equivalent of ten megatons of explosive destruction each time it was fired. The benefit, for the D'lai at least, was there were no after effects that would spoil the planet for an occupying force.

In a conference room on *The Spector*, Negotiator D'iash was conferring with the commanders of the three fleets near Earth, Gathung'l, and Cathar Prime. Each of these handpicked commanders had hundreds of battleships under their direct command, but D'iash was in overall command of not just the invading fleets, but of the entire D'lai Authority.

These three fleets represented nearly a third of the naval forces available to her. The remainder were being held in reserve and would be brought into play once the initial battles had been fought. This particular planet, however, was to be the jewel in D'iash's long term plans.

The fleet was in place in orbit of the planet when D'iash gave the command and the privilege of striking the first blow to her own ship and crew.

"Tactical – destroy the capital city."

A beam of destructive energy launched from a forward turret of *The Spector*. Within seconds the capital city was reduced to rubble. D'iash sincerely hoped that most or all of the government was in the city. A clean decapitation of the government would make the rest of the conquest far easier. The pacifism of her distant cousins was also something she counted on. Unlike the Gathung and the Humans, she expected there to be no resistance of substance from the inhabitants.

"Let's make a few more examples. Order the fleet to fire on designated targets."

One hundred battleships fired upon the defenseless planet, reducing whole cities to fiery waste. D'iash smiled. At her signal, troop carriers began their slow descent to the planet. The next phase of the conquest was underway.

While she was monitoring the progress of the invading army, an aide came close and whispered to her, "Negotiator, we have received news from the Earth fleet."

Turning to the aide, she smiled and said, "Go on."

"As the fleet uncloaked and began to prepare for planetary orbit, Earth... vanished."

Negotiator D'iash stood and shouted, "what do you mean?"

The aide trembled and directed her attention to a wall panel monitoring the three fleets communications and tactical status. D'iash walked to the panel and began flipping through various screens. She settled on one – a view of Earth from the fleet's flagship. Nothing. Where the Earth should be all she saw was a star field. She scrubbed the view backwards in time until she found the time stamp she was looking for. She pressed play. One instant Earth was visible, and the next, it slowly faded from view as something that looked like a force field was covering it up.

"What is this!?" Without Earth, the long laid plans of the D'lai would not get the results she so desperately desired. Their long observations of the planet and its inhabitants were a cause for fear and concern among the D'lai. Humans were scrappy and unlike the peaceful Cathari and the formerly conquered Gathung, D'iash had no idea what the Earth would do if invaded. It was imperative to long-term success that Earth should fall along with Gathung'l and Cathar Prime. D'iash could not leave any loose ends.

Barking orders to several crew members and aides nearby, she demanded that they get to the bottom of this mess. How had Earth disappeared? Did she have help? Could they break it? D'iash needed answers and she needed them now. They had already begun the conquest of Cathar Prime so that would continue.

Gathung'l was leaderless but she dared not pause the attacks. The element of surprise was her best weapon.

D'iash left the bridge and slumped down the corridor to her quarters. She was really feeling her age now.

When she arrived at her quarters and removed her *sdawij*, she avoided glancing in the tall mirror near the entrance. This was one time she did not want to see a hated Cathari face staring back at her. D'iash slouched on a sofa and waited. She also began working on a new plan.

FROM ORBIT, GALLAGHER WHISTLED LOUDLY AS he gazed out one of the broad windows from an observation deck. It was so *odd* to not see Earth in the view but to still see the distant moon orbiting a planet that visually at least was no longer there. He shook his head to clear it. Of course the planet is still there, it's just not *there* as far as anyone off world can tell.

From this vantage point he could not see the distant D'lai fleet had uncloaked from near the Moon. He was thankful that *Atlantis* was cloaked so it could observe but not be vulnerable. On his pad he monitored the planetary cloak. It emitted bursts at frequencies almost undetectable by anyone who didn't know to look for it. The planetary cloak itself was also cloaked in another layer of protection. It would do no good to have it be visible for any enemy to simply shoot out of orbit.

He wondered if the D'lai gathered any intel on the workings of the planetary cloak when they briefly captured *The Avenger*. Even though he worked diligently to keep any data on the prototype separate from the ships main data library, he had been floating around outside when the intruders were rummaging around. He had no idea what would have happened on board and he didn't have the time to find out either.

Gallagher moved to a nearby refreshment station and punched in a code that would deliver him hot tea. Sipping the beverage, he sat at a nearby table and was idly scrolling through his pad when a message came in. He swiped the notification away. He didn't feel like talking to anyone now. Most of the past few years had been dedicated to the cloak and now that it was activated and protecting his home planet, he felt lost and didn't know what would happen next. He finished his tea and was about to turn off the pad and head to his quarters when another message notification popped up. He almost swiped it away but the first few words stopped him in his tracks. "Help me Major – Gathung..."

The notification didn't reveal any more of the message so Gallagher opened it and read it. Rising quickly he was about to go to the bridge when he halted. There was no way the Captain of *Atlantis* was going to agree to let Gallagher leave the ship and go back to a Gathung vessel. Gallagher didn't have any specific orders from Earth but he knew that a Major wouldn't just gallivant around from ship to ship, at least not under standard military protocol.

"Protocol be damned" he said aloud to no one in particular. The room was empty anyway. Thinking rapidly, he devised a plan. He *had* to get to *The Avenger*. Hodges earlier sent an urgent message telling him Gathung'l was under attack and that Kwiu Zig was dead. The message begged Gallagher to help. He and Hodges spent a lot of time together with the Gathung and grew to respect them. Hodges had said there must be *something* they could do. After all, Gathung'l had helped develop the technology that Earth was now hoarding.

Gallagher thought back to when he had been in

Secure Lab Alpha. He guessed that Earth would not be content with just one copy of the device. He had seen the engineers taking detailed readings and he realized they had all the technical schematics at their disposal.

"Hmm... what if... " he mused to himself. "What if they have a copy?"

He sprang into action. He recognized the only two ways off the ship was with permission or sneak off somehow. He couldn't steal a shuttle – those would be closely monitored. What else should he do? Inspiration struck him as remembered what happened with the D'lai ship. Running down the corridor he entered the escape pod bay. He used his knowledge of the ship to simulate a malfunction with one of the pods. He got inside it, strapped in as he had before on *The Spector* and waited. He was thankful that in this pod at least, the seat was designed for a human. He'd programmed a ten-second delay and he counted down silently in his head. With any luck this escape pod would be chalked up to what it looked like – a malfunction.

"Four...three...two...one..." The pod door closed and ejected itself from a launch tube. A second later Gallagher was floating through space. The message from Hodges gave him general coordinates for *The Avenger* in stationary orbit over the cloaked planet. He maneuvered the pod in that direction. It took him almost an hour to get close enough to where the ship was supposed to be.

Now he had to wait. He sent an encoded message but since *The Avenger* was cloaked, he didn't know if they would receive it or not. Hodges had given him instructions that he followed. With any luck, he'd not be stuck in this tin can with nowhere to go.

A few minutes later an indicator light on the control panel lit up. Incoming message. Gallagher opened it and read the two words on the screen. Brace yourself. No sooner had he read the message before the pod was rocked by a loud *thunk* sound outside it. He laughed to himself. Hodges must have attached a tether and was reeling his pod into the cargo bay. After a little time had elapsed, Gallagher realized that he was now inside *The Avenger*'s cargo bay. He stood and checked the pressure indicators. It would do him no good to come all this way and die in a vacuum. The gauges indicated an atmosphere on the other side so he opened the pod and stepped out.

THE BUNKER BELOW UNITED NATIONS headquarters in London was a flurry of activity. Ever since General Cai had activated the planetary cloak and the D'lai had been sighted near the Moon, dozens of governmental ministers and their aides moved in and around the spacious room. Secretary General Allen watched the movement and wondered to herself if some of these people were just doing things to keep active and their minds off of what was going on.

When the Cathari had first come things got crazy fast. This time, their visitors weren't peaceful. They were bent on conquest and not alliances. The world government had spent billions on contingency plans after the initial visits of the Cathari. They'd researched many scenarios and methods of protecting the planet from truly hostile aliens. Earth had developed ever more complex orbital weapon facilities and increased its presence on other worlds in their solar system to reduce the likelihood of complete annihilation of the species.

The planetary cloak was one of the more daring plans and when it had been conceived there was no promise that they would be able to make it a reality. Fortunately, Earth had grown close with Gathung'l and together they began working on the device that each planet intended to use for its own defense. When the D'lai left Gathung'l they left behind a lot of discarded technology that gave an advantage to the Gathung. In addition, the peaceful Cathari had shared much of their own technology with Earth so together the two planets worked in secret for several years on expanding a ship based cloak to the scale of a planet. It was hard work, but for Earth at least, the plan was paying off. The D'lai *knew* the planet was there, they just couldn't do anything at all about it.

Even though Allen was peeved that General Cai had implemented the cloak without her authorization, she was glad that at least for now Earth was not in immediate danger. She of course realized that unlike the American system of government, she was not the "commander-in-chief" but a civilian leader who should be advised and consulted before any military actions were implemented. Allen vowed to have a word in private with the General later, but for now she had more pressing concerns.

"General, what are our next steps?"

"Ma'am, we have another partially completed copy of the cloak and we plan to deploy it, once finished, to protect Mars. There is no sign of D'lai ships near that planet at this time but we also know they have cloaks so it is possible they are out there."

"Do we have naval ships close enough to prepare?"

"Ma'am, *Atlantis* has secondary orders to retrieve the device from the secure lab on the space hub."

"Very good, General." Allen turned to talk a nearby aide about other matters. She turned back to Cai.

"General, what are the contingency plans *on world*?"

"Ma'am, as long as the cloak holds out, life on Earth will continue as if not much has changed. We'll continue to monitor events but we can all relax."

Allen wasn't sure that his smooth reassurances would hold true, but she acquiesced for now. She returned to reviewing the numerous reports flooding her inbox. No one noticed the aide in the corner of the room that was paying a little too much attention to the pace of the room and the discussions between Cai and Allen. None of the humans present in this secure bunker had any idea of the level of infiltration by the D'lai and they did not expect that such a highly placed aide would be spying and recording everything she witnessed.

The spy smiled to herself as she pretended to be working on a report for the Minister of Agriculture. She didn't know yet how she would get this valuable data to the D'lai, but she was prepared for when an opening presented itself. She would not have long to wait.

Interim Leader Bresu Xid was angry at Earth but his primary concern was to protect Gathung'l. He had ordered *The Naomor* to depart from the Sol System and make all available haste back to Gathung'l. He worried that he would be too late and that a D'lai fleet would decimate his home world before he could arrive.

En route, he ordered every Gathung ship in the far-flung Orion Arm to return at once to the Gathung'l system and prepare for conflict with the D'lai. He would be unable to keep the lie in place that the First Dictator was still in charge so he broke with one of Kwiu Zig's most fervent plans and announced the death of Zig to the Gathung people. It would take some time for every ship and Gathung living off planet to get the message, but he hoped that by revealing the truth, he would rally the people around him as he attempted to thwart what he feared would be a new conquest of his planet.

Below decks his engineers and scientists were working feverishly to determine if they had the ability to recreate the planetary cloak. Earth had betrayed the Gathung people but that would be dealt with later. Now, the only thing Xid cared about was keeping the planet and the system as safe as possible.

Gathung'l had no natural moon so the D'lai had not been able to surreptitiously orbit their humongous fleet around one. Instead, they had maintained station at the only other rocky planet in the system. This had the effect of delaying their ability to sneak up on the planet. After the conquest of Gathung'l and after the D'lai had left the system in a doomed attempt to rescue their own civilization, the Gathung had developed and deployed an array of satellites in orbit at the furthest points possible. This mesh like deployment of thousands of devices had the practical effect of preventing any ship without clearance from Gathung'l itself from being cloaked within 100,000 miles of the planets surface.

Naturally the D'lai did not have the authorization so their cloaks would be rendered ineffective as they approached the planet. Therefore, the plan was to move in at maximum speed. Each of the ships in the fleet would approach the planet from slightly different directions so they had a pincer-like effect as they closed in on the surface. The forward turrets of each battleship had a range of 10,000 miles before their destructive power dissipated exponentially.

The commanders of the fleet had war-gamed the invasion hundred of times to plan precise movements and to give themselves as much of the element of surprise as possible. They knew they would be unable to prevent detection, but they hoped that with enough speed and precision of weapon deployments, they would catch the Gathung off guard.

*The Naomor* arrived at Gathung'l just as the D'lai fleet was approaching the outer limits of their cloaking usefulness. Immediately upon arrival in orbit, Xid ordered the planet-wide defensive batteries to activate. His engineers had not been able to come up with a working planetary cloak so that plan would not be useful. Xid feared that his planet could not defend itself forever but he hoped that with enough advance warning it would forestall the inevitable.

The inhabitants of Gathung'l reacted to the news of the First Dictator's death and the coming invasion by the D'lai in typical Gathung behavior. Those who remembered the previous occupation put into action their own plans to survive the coming disaster. The Gathung had never been a race that lived in vast metropolitan cities but they had de-urbanized even more after the occupation. It was not unusual for an ordinary Gathung to live a mile from their nearest neighbor. This sparseness was a strength that Interim Leader Xid was counting on. The planetary defense batteries would no doubt take out at least a portion of the attacking fleet and the D'lai could not simply destroy a heavily populated center on the planet in the hopes of destabilizing the system.

It would be a long battle but the D'lai were confident of their eventual success. A miracle would be required to save Gathung'l now.

PART 3

# PART III - THE BATTLE FOR SURVIVAL

# CHAPTER 9

Gallagher was met on *The Avenger* by Hodges. The pair wasted no time with talking and headed instead to the bridge to brief Captain Ziqna. All eyes turned to the men when they entered the room. Ziqna, for his part, continued a muted discussion with a military aide. As soon as he concluded, he turned to Gallagher.

"Major. What is all this?"

"Captain, we don't have time to waste. We need to go to Saturn."

"Saturn? Are you mad? My orders are to return to Gathung'l at once," said the Captain. "I don't have time for detours."

Gallagher and Hodges told the Captain of their plan. They believed the secure lab had another copy of the planetary cloak and Gallagher hoped they would obtain it and protect Gathung'l in time. Ziqna listened with interest but he was unconvinced.

"Captain, an incoming message from Interim Leader Xid."

"Put it on speaker."

There was a slight crackle and then Xid's voice blared throughout the bridge.

"This is Interim Leader Bresu Xid to any Gathung ship receiving this message," the voice began. "The D'lai have begun aerial bombardment of the planet. Half of our defensive batteries have been rendered useless by D'lai agents on the ground. There is no time to waste, we need..." The voice ended abruptly. Ziqna ordered his communications officer to get the message back at once. It was to no avail. The message had been cut off mid sentence and try as she might, the communications officer could not obtain it.

Ziqna turned to Gallagher and Hodges. "You are *certain* we can get a cloak?"

Gallagher nodded. "Well, I'm about 80% certain. I know there is another one, I'm just not sure I can steal it."

"You will have every available person on this ship at your disposal," said Ziqna. "Get us that cloak!"

*The Avenger* set course and traveled to Saturn. It would take them three hours to travel there and everyone on the bridge prayed it would not be too late. Gallagher looked at Hodges, no smile on his face. Instead, he had a look of uncertainty that made Hodges feel very scared indeed.

IN ORBIT AROUND CATHAR PRIME, NEGOTIATOR D'iash reviewed logs from the capture and release of *The Avenger*. She felt certain they had missed something. She read the Gathung crew was traveling back and forth between Earth and Gathung'l regularly. There must be a reason. She had been briefed on secret plans by her spy aboard *The Avenger* but that spy did not have specific details.

The Gathung Captain and the Human engineers had kept things very compartmentalized and the actual secret was not in the ships main database that had been copied during the brief takeover. She was about to give up and move on when she decided on a whim to review security footage that had been captured by her agents that had boarded the ship. She scrolled through the images and then something caught her eye. She scrubbed back and found it. A small hangar bay with what looked like a wide and bulky satellite. The grainy image didn't reveal what exactly it was, but D'iash hoped she had found something useful.

The D'lai maintained a vast database of every encounter with every ship and civilization. Buried somewhere in this database was all the sensor logs from the capture of *The Avenger*. D'iash didn't have the technical expertise to drill down on all that data but she had someone on board that might. She set her analyst to work and went back to reviewing reports. The conquest of Cathar Prime was going well and at any time she should receive an update on the re-conquest of Gathung'l. The puzzle of what to do about Earth frustrated her. She reviewed mission plans for that particular system and reeled in shock as she found a glaring omission.

The fleet was attacking *only* the Earth. Humans had made a huge push to colonize their entire system and had inhabitants on Mars and Titan. Smaller fleets were poised to take those two smaller worlds. The mission plans did not include the space hub. D'iash immediately contacted the commander of the Sol system fleet.

"Commander, *why* are we not preparing to attack the Saturn space hub?"

The commander reeled for a moment and then reviewed his notes.

"Negotiator, the hub is small and was deemed as non-essential to overall system objectives."

"Who made *that* determination?"

The commander paused, then said, "Negotiator... *you* ordered us to ignore it."

D'iash swore and closed the channel. She was slipping. She stormed around her office. Her disbelief in her own faulty judgement call forced her to call into question the entire plan she had so carefully laid out after the destruction of her home system. She felt so stupid.

She attempted to calm herself to no avail. Signs of weakness in leadership among her people could be a fatal miscalculation and she sensed it. She began plotting how she would spin this lapse in judgement and how she might make up for it. Negotiator D'iash needed to move quickly. No doubt the commander of the Sol system fleet would wonder what had just happened and the word would begin to spread that she was forgetting key components that would mean the difference between success and failure.

Cathar Prime was in chaos. With the swift removal of the planetary government and hundreds of thousands of D'lai troops now landing and planning on occupying key facilities on the planet, the Cathari cowered in their homes and places of business, unsure how to proceed or even how to fight back.

The peaceful society faced its greatest threat since the D'lai had been banished from the planet after the last major upheaval. No one living remembered the circumstances and even fewer learned of the actions that set this entire plan into motion a thousand years in the past.

Regional leaders in cities that had not yet been destroyed completely worked to calm their own people but the D'lai were brutal in conquest. While ordinary Cathari attempted to keep out of the way of the invaders, prominent Cathari were being rounded up. They remembered how the D'lai had dealt with the far less docile Gathung and the people hoped this would not be the same. They were wrong.

The D'lai hatred of the Cathari was so ingrained that soldiers took real joy at destroying and killing as much as possible. In orbit, the bombardment of population centers continued unabated killing one third of the planet's inhabitants in the first twelve hours of the invasion.

While most of the orbital facilities and space ships had been destroyed or rendered useless during the invasion, a few ships had managed to cloak, thereby hiding themselves and providing an opportunity to record and report on the heavy destruction. One such ship, *The Manchester*, operated under less than legal registry and kept itself cloaked as much as possible. On board, the Captain, a thirty-five year old human called Zea Windrow, watched in terror as the bombardment of the planet continued.

*The Manchester* was engaging in some small-time smuggling between a Cathari wine merchant and a Scree governor when the D'lai appeared in the skies above Cathar Prime. Zea had just picked up a shipment of wine from the planet and was ordering her navigator to take them to the FTL injection coordinates. The presence of the massive fleet disrupted her ship's navigation and she was thankful it had. She had no idea if the invaders detected a cloaked ship and she had no intention of being a victim.

"All stop!" Zea ordered. "Tactical, find us an opening in that fleet so we can move the hell out of here."

Bridge officers worked to find an escape route. The presence of so many vessels disrupting local space would make leaving orbit very difficult indeed. Several tense minutes passed as the crew attempted to plot a course. Zea decided it might be historically important for someone to keep a record of the invasion of the peaceful planet. She didn't know who exactly the invaders were, but their sheer level of organization and size meant they would not be deterred by a small smuggling ship.

"Captain, I've found a small opening and have given the coordinates to the navigator."

"Very good. Navigation, how long until we are out of here?"

The navigator checked his panel. "Ma'am, with the incredible number of battleships nearby, it will take us... " he paused, "um... twelve hours to sneak past."

Zea sighed and sat back. "Well, do what we can. Let's mark this all down in our logs. The data might be useful to someone, somewhere."

*The Manchester* moved slowly, keeping maximum distance from each of the massive ships. She did not want there to be even the slightest sign she was out here. Zea Windrow had no intention of joining the Cathari in the grave.

THE AVENGER DOCKED WITH THE SATURN SPACE hub three hours after leaving Earth. Captain Ziqna was sure he would be denied docking and was shocked that out here, this far from Earth, it appeared to be business as usual. He informed Major Gallagher and Engineer Hodges that docking was complete and hoped they would be able to find something useful from the secure lab.

Ziqna had spent the past few years learning how the humans operated. Where a typical Gathung could be clever and deceptive in obtaining whatever it is he was after, these humans were *cunning*. They seemed to have a knack at getting their way even when everything else looked on the surface to be disaster. Ziqna understood Gallagher was not an ordinary engineer and was placed on his ship by Earth's military leadership. At first he had been displeased at the posting but he soon learned how useful it was to have him on board.

During an early mission between the two planets, the ship had entered a pocket of space that rendered their FTL drive useless. Navigation computers projected the area to be enormous enough that it would take *The Avenger* six months to traverse using only engine thrusters. Ziqna had resigned himself and his crew to a much longer than anticipated voyage. Gallagher, on the other hand, refused to accept this state of affairs and worked night and day for almost a week devising a plan to escape this spatial anomaly. Gallagher had discovered the region was particularly dense with dark matter and this matter interfered with the FTL drive which required much lower density space to operate. He actually almost reinvented FTL drive to work in high density areas and cut the six-month delay down by 90%. What would take any other ship over 180 days to traverse took *The Avenger* just 18 days.

This new iteration of the FTL drive was now standard on Gathung and Earth ships. Leadership of both planets determined they would not include this new development in the ongoing technology swapping between the Cathari Alliance and the nonaligned Earth. They wanted to keep this as their own secret weapon. A side benefit of the newly developed FTL modification was it aided them in development of the planetary cloak.

Ordinary cloaking devices had a maximum output based on the size of the ship they were designed for. Hiding an entire planet was a technological feat that most Earth and Gathung scientists discarded as pure science fiction. Using the calculations Gallagher had come up with enabled the ability to expand the cloak exponentially. Ziqna would never again question Major Gallagher in any of his schemes. The out of the box thinking saved not only his own crew, but might potentially now be the salvation for his entire race.

Gallagher and Hodges found the secure lab empty. Gallagher was furious they had come all this way and the mission would be a failure. If Gathung could not put its hands on a planetary cloak, it might as well surrender. The far superior D'lai forces would sweep aside their defenses and resume the occupation that had created so many problems the last time around.

Hodges was about to give up and tell Gallagher they needed to return to the ship when Gallagher had a flash of inspiration.

"Wait a sec buddy," said Gallagher. "The last time I was here, I had override codes. I was monitoring the prototype and I needed access."

"Well, fingers crossed then!"

Gallagher input his override codes into the key pad and waited. Nothing. He tried a second time and still nothing happened. Swearing to himself, he saw that the small indicator lights on the keypad didn't light up as he input the code.

"Duh..." He said to himself.

Hodges chuckled. "No power."

Hodges was an expert engineer and he always had a plan for when things went wrong. He searched the area and found a stanchion that was being used to divide the small reception room. Grabbing it, he moved to the wall near the keypad. He studied for a moment and then without warning Gallagher, began hammering at the wall panel.

Gallagher jumped back in surprise but soon realized what Hodges was doing. He had made a small opening in the wall, revealing a jumble of wires. Hodges used a battery pack and a pair of pliers and together created enough of a power circuit that the keypad came to life. Gallagher entered the override code once more and the entrance to the secure facility swished open.

"I sure hope the rest of this so-called secure facility is a little more secure," said Hodges.

Gallagher laughed as the pair waded deeper into the dark lab. Gallagher remembered the floor plan of the lab and using his comm device as a flashlight, led Hodges to the small area adjacent to the clean room. Hodges had to work his magic with the stanchion once more and both men entered.

"Well, I guess we don't have to worry about keeping things tidy," said Gallagher.

"No one home to be mad at us," replied Hodges.

They searched the room and found what they were looking for. The team at the secure lab had not had enough time to replicate the prototype, but the bare bones of one was here. Gallagher signaled Ziqna to send some men with a lot of muscles to come help them before they were detected. Minutes later three bear-sized Gathung crew members pushing a hover-cart entered the clean room. Together the three Gathung and two humans got the unwieldy device onto the cart and had almost made it to the exit when alarms began to blare.

"Uh...we'd better run," shouted Gallagher over the noise.

The five of them rushed down the corridors and were able to board *The Avenger* without any further problems. Ziqna was at first ecstatic with the recovered technology but then when he saw the state of it he fretted. Gallagher and Hodges assured the Captain that they would get it into working order.

"How long until this *ḍawi kia voi* is functional?"

Gallagher smirked at the Captains use of vulgarity. "We will have to... um... borrow a few things but we should be able to make it functional in oh... 36 hours," said Hodges.

"Just get it done," said Ziqna. "I don't know how much time we have left until everything is lost."

The two men got down to work, hoping they had what they needed to complete the task. Only time and a lot of sweat would tell.

Most humans on Earth had no idea that anything significant had occurred. The cloak was not visible from the surface except for a hardly noticeable dip in sunlight on the daylight side of the planet. Nearly everyone went about their business working, playing, sleeping, having sex, and generally enjoying life post-war and secure in the knowledge that all was right in the galaxy.

On Mars, things were more confused. Martian leadership fretted over the loss of communications from Earth. It wasn't entirely uncommon that something as simple as a solar flare disrupted links between the two planets, however the absence of increased solar output forced planetary leadership to consider the alternatives and none of them were promising.

Mars had developed its own planetary government that was separate from the United Nations on Earth. Even though both planets were occupied by humans with a small scattering of extra terrestrials, conditions on the two planets could not be more different. On Earth, people came and went as they pleased without worry; on Mars even a tiny crack spelled disaster for the jumbo habitats and modules that had been erected and enlarged in the years since colonization began.

Martian Leader Jose Arroyo was almost militaristic in his attempts to keep the citizens of the planet safe and functioning smoothly. The loss of communication with Earth was seriously troubling. He ordered his aides to find out what was going on and waited impatiently while they searched for clues.

"Sir, communications links with Earth stopped just as we were transmitting the latest scientific data to the Dyson Institute," said an aide.

The Dyson Institute was developing plans to fully terraform the planet and had commissioned an epic study to seek out the use of Mars natural resources. Small areas of the planet had been pseudo-terraformed but those areas remained under voluminous domes to keep atmosphere in and to prevent damage from solar radiation due to Mars thin atmosphere and absence of a magnetic field.

Arroyo was among the first generation of Martians who had been born on the planet from parents who had also been born on Mars. He had never been to Earth and considered the red planet to be home. He had served the Martian people in one role or another since he graduated from college and after a time, serving in the planetary legislature, he had been elected Prime Minister of Mars. The only trouble was, he was elected as Prime Minister last week and this was the first crisis of his tenure. He had surrounded himself with knowledgeable people but so far as he could tell, no one had ever had to deal with a total loss of communications from the home planet on this scale before.

After several hours of theorizing and trying different frequencies, a scientific advisor ran into the room and knocked over a chair in his haste. Prime Minister Arroyo turned to the clumsy man.

"Lukas, calm down!"

"I can't Sir," replied Lukas, "I've discovered why we can't contact Earth." He paused, breathless and then continued. "Earth is *gone!*"

The room fell silent. "What do you mean gone?" Asked the Prime Minister.

"We can't see it on telescopes or any other device. However, we don't believe the planet has been destroyed. The moon seems to still be in its expected orbit."

Arroyo was puzzled. How could Earth not be there but its absence seemed to make no difference to other celestial bodies.

"Could the Earth somehow be *cloaked*?"

"That is one possible explanation," replied Lukas. "We'll do some more investigation, sir."

"Very good," said the Prime Minister. His attention was diverted to other matters but he had a feeling this was going to preoccupy him until the mystery was solved.

In space, a small fleet of D'lai ships approached the planet quietly. This time, they kept their cloaks in place and waited. No one on Mars had any idea of what would come next.

COMMANDER D'SHAN SAT AT HIS communications panel in thought long after he had spoken with the Negotiator. He was concerned that she seemed to have forgotten the commands she had personally issued regarding the Sol system and he wondered aloud to himself if she had made other mistakes.

He reached out to other commanders surreptitiously to see if they had noticed any lapses themselves. While he waited for further information, he decided the time was now to move some of his idle battleships into position near Earth's other solar system outposts. He sent three small fleets to Mars, Titan, and Saturn. This was against the well-defined protocol in place, but he also realized that the success of this mission depended on his leadership. He was not going to let an aging Negotiator ruin the plans.

One characteristic of the D'lai, as well as the much more docile Cathari, is the ability to form plans within plans. Commander D'shan was part of a small cabal of D'lai leaders that formed a secret shadow government and was ready to jump into action at the moment that they sensed success might be had. The current structure of power among the disparate and homeless D'lai was top-heavy and one person, in this case the Negotiator herself, could ruin everything with negligence or senility. D'shan felt sure this wasn't a case of not doing a task. He hoped it wasn't senility. He had no idea that Negotiator D'iash was herself suffering from the beginning ravages of extreme old age and in time, she would not be able to continue at all.

Even though the Cathari and the D'lai had parted ways centuries in the past, they still shared the same DNA and afflictions. Even though most D'lai thought of themselves as a separate species from the Cathari, they were in fact genetically almost identical. Some changes had developed as the two civilizations evolved, but not enough time had passed for there to be any major changes. The only real change was skin color. The D'lai spent their entire lives aboard ships so their skin was much more pale than the Cathari who had a magnificent sun shining on them all day, every day. Those few D'lai who had survived the supernova did have slightly denser pigmentation, but even that began to fade.

D'shan read a few messages that came in from others in his cabal. The consensus seemed to be that the time was incredibly near when they would seize power in a coup and take power from D'iash and her flunkies. The cabal had members in almost every ship in each of the three major attacking fleets. Their goal was simple – they would finish what she started. The only exception was that they would not just settle for *three* planets. The D'lai cabal wanted *every* inhabited planet. The galaxy belonged to them and they would take it.

D'shan sent encoded replies telling his compatriots to prepare and be ready to implement their plan on short notice. In the meantime, he had to fine tune his own plans for conquering Sol and enslaving humanity. Humans were weak and they would make excellent chattel in the coming galactic conflict.

D'shan smiled broadly and stood. He walked purposefully to his bridge and gave the orders to move in. He was done waiting for Negotiator Ret D'iash.

ONE HAZARD OF WAR IS ONE NATION OR civilization spying on another. The D'lai were experienced at spy craft and made it a major component of any invasion plan to position spies or to recruit spies as part of their prep work. Placing spies on Earth was a challenge owing to the fact that the planet had limited the total number of aliens allowed on the planet at one time. Cathar Prime was the easiest to infiltrate because the D'lai simply placed a member of their own race in plain sight.

Paula Fister started out her adult life as a communications officer working in the office of the Minister of Agriculture in London. She lived a relatively ordinary life but she had a huge secret. She worried constantly that others would find out that when she was thirteen years old, she had been involved with an older boy and together they held up a small convenience store in a desperate bid to have enough money to attend a local concert of their favorite band. It was a stupid move and her boyfriend had been killed in the attempt. Paula escaped and spent the last twenty years praying she would not be caught.

Paula knew that she was technically a murderer and feared the repercussions. She was amazed that she managed to hide her crime for so long. One afternoon she was cycling home on a rented bike from the Ministry to the tube for her twenty-five minute ride from Liverpool Street Station to Barking. She could not afford the pricier rents closer to the Ministry and so this daily commute was just part of her routine.

She had just been about to swipe and enter the tube station when a man walked up behind her and grabbed her. She was whirled around and as she faced her attacker, she was struck by his fine, handsome face. He whisked her away from the turnstiles in a strong grip she was unable to break free of. As she was about to let out a scream, he silenced her with a look that frightened her.

"Scream and you're mum is dead."

"That hurts!"

"You and I need to have a small talk, don't we?" The man held on to her arm but kept his voice low.

"Follow me, yeah, and no harm comes to her." He then proceeded to give the exact address where her mother lived in a small house near Windsor as proof of his power over her.

Paula gave up and agreed. She followed the man up the escalator and out into the bright sunlight of an unseasonably warm London summer day. He led her to a small pub that at this hour was almost empty. Ordering two pints, he sat her down in a corner and stared at her.

Paula felt tears in her eyes but she was too frightened to show her emotion. The man kept staring at her as he pushed a pint in her direction.

"You are going to need that I believe." He spoke in a rather posh accent which surprised her. She'd have figured that some common street thug who kidnaps innocent women from the tube station would be barely able to speak at all.

"I know what you did when you were a young girl," he began. Paula's eyes showed her shock at the statement. "Now, Miss Fister, you are going to follow my directions precisely, or you will be turned over to Scotland Yard and your dear old mum will find herself dead and floating in the Thames."

"I don't know what you mean by..." Paula said.

"Don't bloody lie to me Miss." He patted his coat pocket. "I have a CCTV recording of the whole murderous scene."

Paula shook her head in silent agreement. "What do you want me to do?"

"You will use this thumb drive," he said passing her the small drive, "and you will deliver to me on Tuesday all the data on projected crop yields for the coming fiscal year."

Paula looked at him, shocked. "Why would you want that? Just wait a month and it will be public!" She started to rise from the chair but he grabbed her and yanked her back down.

"You will do as you are asked or you'll find out what English justice does to murdering bitches like you."

After a little more persuasion in which he showed her live footage of her aged mother pruning roses in her front garden, Paula agreed. She left the pub in shock and couldn't figure out for the life of her why the man wanted such mundane data. She vowed to do it anyway. She had no desire to spend the rest of her days locked in some women's prison.

Still in the pub, the man smiled to himself. Conditioning an unwilling spy was a lot of fun and he looked forward to the time he would be able to gather real intelligence from the unsuspecting fool Paula Fister. He sent a short text message via an encoded app to report on his progress. He finished both pints and left the pub.

"RED ALERT! ALL HANDS TO BATTLE STATIONS!" Ordered Captain Ziqna as *The Avenger* fled the vicinity of the Saturn space hub. Their presence on the hub had not gone unnoticed and they were currently being chased by a much larger Earth battleship.

Ziqna had been unable to order his ship to cloak after leaving the hub. The attacking ship was using a disruption beam that painted the ship with charged particles that prevented a cloak from bending the light around the ship. Unless he could maneuver out of range, he didn't see how he would move to safety. The smaller ship was much more maneuverable but the battleship made up for that agility with speed.

The two ships raced past the surface of the distant Saturn in a struggle that would determine the fate of Gathung'l itself. Engineer Hodges was giving everything he had to coax more speed out of *The Avenger* and they routed all power, including some of the life support and gravity, to the thrusters.

Gallagher tried to help Hodges but this was out of his comfort zone. He furiously racked his brain for a solution. He had stolen a piece of technology that Earth wanted for itself, but he could not sit by and watch as another friendly world was ravaged by the D'lai. He wondered if his access codes for the Secure Lab would be of any help in this crisis. He couldn't see how the two systems would work together, but he also remembered that the military liked to reuse and recycle as much as they could. He figured it wouldn't hurt so he sat down at a communications panel and opened a terminal window. He wrote some rough code that could send a short burst to the attacking ship. He thought he might be able to use the disruption beam itself so the incoming message would look like background noise and not be seen as a threat.

Working feverishly, Gallagher came up with some untested code and after he transferred it to an active comm window, he input his override code and pressed send. He whooped when the reply came back from the battleship asking him for a command. He searched the systems command functions and found the one he was looking for. Crossing his fingers behind his back he sent the command to disable the disruption beam for 60 seconds. When he received a confirmation he jumped from his chair and shouted. *The Avenger* only had 60 seconds so he quickly informed the Captain.

On the bridge, Ziqna ordered the ship to cloak and for navigation to use a preprogrammed evasion pattern. With any luck they might cloak and change position so the huge battleship could not find them. After a few tense seconds, confirmation came back.

"Cloak successfully activated. Engaging evasion pattern alpha."

The star field outside the window changed and Ziqna ordered a distance reading to be counted off. They needed to be ten kilometers from the battleship before they would be safe from the disruption beam. Ziqna sighed in relief when they reached the safe limit.

"Navigator, set course at once for the alternate FTL injection point. Take us to Gathung'l."

Navigator Arvesp Erth happily complied. They couldn't risk being caught at the routine FTL site for fear the humans would be there waiting for them.

With any luck, they'd arrive at the new injection point in less than an hour and be able to jump to Gathung'l.

"Hang tight everyone, we are coming." Arvesp said to herself. The rest of the crew no doubt shared her sentiment.

While everyone on the bridge was cheerful at their escape from the close call with the battleship, a somber communications officer turned in his seat to face the Captain.

"Captain," said the officer. "We have just received a coded communication from Interim Leader Xid, on Gathung'l."

"Put it on speaker."

"This is Interim Leader Bresu Xid in orbit of Gathung'l. An hour ago a giant fleet of D'lai battleships uncloaked inside our cloaking dispersal field. I have ordered all planetary and orbital weapon arrays to fire on the fleet. We have launched countermeasures and sent into orbit billions of metallic cubes capable of damaging or even destroying any landing vessels. At this time no ship can leave or land on Gathung'l without serious risk. We will not take this invasion at anything less than our full strength. At the present time none of the D'lai ships have fired on the planet. Any available ship within ten light years of

Gathung'l is being recalled to assist in planetary defense. May the gods have mercy on our people. Xid out."

"Navigator, how long until we have reached insertion?"

Arvesp checked her display. "Sir, less than 10 minutes."

"Punch all available power to the engines. We need to go to Gathung'l, now."

Minutes later *The Avenger* arrived at the FTL insertion point. The crew didn't detect any other ships in the vicinity so Ziqna ordered the ship to uncloak and prepare to jump. As soon as the ship was uncloaked, proximity alarms went off on the bridge. *The Avenger* shuddered as a tractor beam was locked onto the hull and the ship was dragged into the cargo bay of the Earth battleship they thought they evaded.

The tactical officer turned to Captain Ziqna to inform him of intruders on board the ship but he didn't have to. A second later a dozen armed and shielded humans stormed the deck.

"Captain Ziqna of Gathung'l," said the lead human, "this ship is under impound by the authority of the United Nations of Earth. Your crew is to be detained." The officer continued, "where is Major Cormac Gallagher?"

Ziqna sat in his command chair and put his head in his hands. It was all over. Gathung'l would now surely fall to the D'lai. For the first time in his life, Ziqna was actually crying.

## CHAPTER 10

Major Gallagher reflected on recent events from a holding cell on Titan. Hours earlier he had been attempting to build a planetary cloak for Gathung'l when the ship had been captured and everyone detained. He didn't assume that his ploy to get the disruption beam disabled would go unnoticed, but he hadn't expected the same battleship to *know* where *The Avenger* would head to try to jump home.

He expected a long and drawn out interrogation and he was surprised when he was brought to a small, windowless room with nothing but a chair and an outsized display monitor on the wall. Gallagher shrugged and sat in the metal chair and waited. He didn't wait long. The screen came to life and he was face to face with none other than Secretary General Marsha Allen.

"Major Gallagher," said Allen. "I understand you've stolen something from us?"

"Um yes Ma'am," said Gallagher, "but Ma'am, you weren't using it at the moment."

Allen actually laughed before continuing. "As you are no doubt aware, Earth is under siege from a massive D'lai fleet. We are cloaked and safe and... "

"Excuse me Ma'am, but *how* are you talking to me? I thought communications weren't possible behind the cloak."

"Gallagher, do you think we would allow ourselves to be entirely helpless?"

"No offense Ma'am but I helped design that cloak and I..."

"Major, time is of the essence and I need to be direct with you."

Gallagher didn't have any retort so he remained quiet.

"It is true, the cloak prevents *most* communication frequencies that are in common usage, but my staff has found a way to tunnel through the cloak using lasers to send a signal past the cloak that bounces off something or other. I really don't understand the mechanics. Just suffice to say it works."

"Yes, Ma'am," replied Gallagher.

"Anyway, I also understand it was your intention to take the stolen property to Gathung'l in a desperate attempt to save them?"

"Well it was desperate. The tech I stole wasn't functional and I was hoping to…"

"Yes, I know all that. The captain of *Atlantis* filled me in. I make it a point to never ask a question I don't know the answer to."

Gallagher smiled. He liked this lady.

"Now, I need you to continue what you were doing. Get that cloak working but it can't go to Gathung'l Major, it has to be deployed around Mars."

"But… this cloak was supposed to go to Gathung'l, they helped us build it!"

"I know Major. Mars also needs it and we only have *one* device to use. I'm not Solomon!"

"Respectfully, Ma'am, I can't…"

"Major, if you are going to say you *can't* do something, let me stop you. Stealing the cloaking device," she held up a hand to stop any more responses from Gallagher, "even a non-functioning one, is an act of war." She paused a moment, "an act of war we take *very* seriously."

Gallagher was stunned they would consider the defense of another planet, an ally, to be an act of war.

"At least as far as General Cai and the military is concerned," said Allen. "I'm concerned for the well-being of fellow *humans*. Humans on a planet with almost no atmosphere where one good shot will take down their entire ecosystem."

The screen crackled and Allen disappeared. When she returned, she said, "this conversation has gone on too long. Gallagher, get that cloak to Mars. Do it now or face the consequences."

The communication ended and left Gallagher shaken. He did want to help his fellow humans but he also was desperate to help his friends on Gathung'l also. This was one of those no-win scenarios where you are damned if you do and damned if you don't. If he saved Mars, Gathung'l was dead. If he saved Gathung'l, Mars was dead. He had no idea what he was going to do but he needed to decide soon. Millions of lives depended on his answer.

In orbit around Cathar Prime, Negotiator D'iash read the communication from her commander of the Sol fleet. Earth found a way to communicate through its cloak that sent her science team racing to find a way to use that same ability to perhaps break the cloak or at least weaken it. It was frustrating that the cloak tricked all the fleet's weapons and sensors into thinking Earth is gone. The D'lai had to find a way to break it or their plans would be moot.

D'iash dug once more through the records from the capture of *The Avenger*. She now had a name to go with this treachery – Major Cormac Gallagher. The very same Gallagher *someone* in her own crew helped escape *The Spector* only days earlier. While she scoured the capture logs she had her security staff searching for the wretched traitor.

One section of the logs kept her coming back over and over. There was a small cargo hold that held some kind of satellite or orbital device. She presumed that would be the planetary cloak. She studied the image and the metadata. D'iash noticed a small tag associated with the image and froze. She found it! The device was giving off a very low level frequency everyone including herself missed.

D'iash opened communications with Sol.

"Commander D'shan, I'm sending you a frequency. I want you to use it to see if you can retrain your sensors to detect Earth."

"Yes, Negotiator... receiving it now."

The Negotiator paced her quarters impatiently. Five minutes later the voice of the Commander came back.

"Negotiator! Sensors detect an enormous gravity source. We can't *see* Earth but we can detect her gravity!"

It was a start. "Commander D'shan, use every available resource. Fine tune it and let's see where that leads us!

"Yes Negotiator."

D'iash returned to her thoughts while she waited for updates on breaking through the cloak. She was furious no one in the vast D'lai network of spies reported this technology was being developed.

The conquest of Cathar Prime was proceeding well and within a day or two it should be complete. At least that pleased the Negotiator. D'iash reflected on why exactly leaders of her civilization were called

Negotiator. The exact origins had been lost to the centuries, but she believed in the early days of D'lai conquest, her forebears attempted to negotiate surrender instead of taking what they wanted by force.

Current plans did not leave any room for negotiating with the Cathari or any other civilization. D'iash believed her military force to be far superior to that of any other race and the cloak was incredibly frustrating for her. It was a piece of tech her own people should have created, not the simple humans or the submissive Gathung.

Tremors shook her body and they forced her to recline on her bed until they passed. The extreme old age that was ravaging her body would soon leave her unable to continue as Negotiator and D'iash knew soon she would not be able to hide it. She waited for the symptoms to fade. She had only months at best. Everything was at stake and she was desperate to finish what she started. Cathar Prime *must* be destroyed and the aborted work she started on Gathung'l tortured her.

D'iash slipped into a feverish sleep and dreamed of childhood on D'lai. Ordinarily she slept in fits and starts but this sleep was deep. She slept so soundly she missed the communications alert that came in. D'shan had news. The Negotiator would not receive it for several hours and by then, control of the D'lai Authority may have slipped straight out of her hands.

BRESU XID MAINTAINED ORBIT AROUND Gathung'l as he waited for reinforcements to appear. His desperate message to all Gathung ships resulted in hundreds of arrivals. Those ships capable of cloaking were ordered to high stationary orbits while those without cloaks were kept in abeyance near one of the other planets in the system. His hope was to use a pincer-like movement to trap the D'lai fleet between the dangerous low orbit and prevent them from also escaping.

Already, three D'lai ships had been destroyed when they attempted to land. The minefield of debris he set loose in orbit did its job and now those three dead ships just added to the hazards. The debris field would pose a flight hazard for any vessels but he would clean that mess up later.

Scientists aboard *The Naomor* and other ships had been working non-stop to recreate the planetary

cloak to no avail. Earth kept the most important specifications to itself and with *The Avenger* now in the
custody of the humans, logs could not be obtained
either. The compartmentalization that had been
employed to keep enemies unaware of the tech had
also been the undoing of the tech. Planetary defenses
would have to suffice but Xid hoped a breakthrough
would come and he would hide his planet before the
D'lai figured out how to survive the orbital debris
field.

Captain Ziqna sent a communications burst to the
Gathung home world just prior to the capture of his
ship. He included data regarding the D'lai capture of
his craft as well as sensory data from the successful
test of the cloak near the moon Ganymede. Xid
possessed a few more tricks and he intended to use
them while he waited for a breakthrough.

He studied crew manifests for all the ships that
did not possess cloaks. He thought if he could get a
few of them to fly on autopilot near Gathung'l he
might trick the D'lai into thinking a full attack was
underway. He would use those decoys to lure as many
of the D'lai battleships as possible away from
Gathung'l.

After the D'lai left, the First Dictator in a stroke

of genius ordered that in addition to the cloak dispersal field around the planet, that a minefield be built in orbit of one of the large gas giant's moons. Everyone at the time thought he was nuts to put the minefield so far from the home planet, but Kwiu Zig insisted that it would be used as a backup plan in case one was ever needed.

The minefield was cloaked but the mines were magnetic. Even if a cloaked ship passed through the minefield, the mines themselves would be drawn to the ship. A cloak prevents visible and ultraviolet light from interacting with a ship, but it doesn't change the laws of physics when it comes to magnetism and gravity.

Xid hoped he might lure the D'lai to that moon and destroy at least a handful of them in the mine-field. He opened a coded communications channel to five ships with small crew complements. He ordered them to transfer their crews to other nearby ships and instructed them on setting up their navigation computers so they would attract the attention of the invaders.

Six hours after the plans had been implemented, his own ships sensors detected the small fleet approaching the planet. The plan was to keep them half an astronomical unit away from Gathung'l and far enough away from the D'lai that they would get a head start in escaping. Xid understood that these ships would not indefinitely escape and that the more advanced D'lai battleships would pursue them with greater speed. His scientists calculated as many variables as possible and with any luck, the D'lai ships would be trapped in the minefield and destroyed or at least severely damaged.

Xid and his crew stared intently as the maneuvers played out. Using satellite data he was able to track the ships and he was relieved that the D'lai dispatched twenty of their battleships in the cat and mouse game. All the ships soon passed out of range of sensors. The decoy ships had been programmed to transmit coded communications when they were within range of the gas giant. It took four and a half hours to travel at full speed from Gathung'l to the gas giant. When four hours passed Xid could not stand it any longer and he began to pace his bridge. Every few minutes he checked the chronometer and looked over at his tactical officer for an update. Thirty seven minutes later, an incoming message arrived from three of the five ships. The D'lai destroyed two of them en route after they had problems with their engines and lost speed. The remaining three in the small fleet had been successful and reached the gas giant ahead of the twenty D'lai ships.

Satellites out near the minefield recorded what happened next and Xid ordered the replay on the bridges main viewer. He sat back and watched as the three Gathung ships and D'lai ships one by one imploded as mines were drawn to them and destroyed them. All twenty ships of the D'lai were obliterated. With the three orbital ships that had been destroyed near Gathung'l and now these twenty, that left another seventy-seven ships to deal with.

Now all Xid and the Gathung had to do was figure out ways to keep picking away at the remaining fleet.

GENERAL CAI STORMED INTO MARSHA ALLEN'S office accompanied by ten armed soldiers. Earlier he intercepted the communication between the Secretary General and Major Gallagher and was enraged at the betrayal. He was the Commander-in-Chief of *Earth* and not of Mars or Saturn. While he was sympathetic to the plight of other humans elsewhere in the galaxy, his sole mission was to protect Earth. Any cloaking technology was meant for that reason alone. Beside that, the fact that the Secretary General found a way to break the communications blackout endangered everything he was working towards. He decided the time was now to take full control of the planet *and* its government.

Allen was reading a document on her console when the General intruded. "General, what can I..." she paused when she saw the armed escort.

"Secretary General Marsha Allen, you are hereby being detained and removed from office."

Allen stood up, furious. "Detained? On what authority?"

"Mine, *Ma'am,*" he retorted. "You have betrayed your oath and I am taking charge of this planet."

"General Cai, what are you talking about?"

"You sent coded communications to Saturn, breaking our blackout. You arranged to use secret technology in defense of another planet..."

"Another planet? You mean a planet where *humans* live?"

"This planet is your concern, not Mars, not Saturn, not aliens."

Allen started to protest further but Cai silenced

her. "I am taking interim command. You will be held in your quarters until such time as a trial can be held and if found guilty of this treason you are executed."

A defiant Marsha Allen went with the troops. She pushed one of the soldiers away when he tried to grasp her arm. As she was being led out from her own office, she nodded to one of her nearby aides. Cai underestimated Marsha Allen. She had often been described as a scrapper and she prearranged plans for just such an attempted coup.

The aide nodded silently back and in the confusion of the arrest he was able to slip out of the outer office and into an adjacent corridor. He ran down the long hall and entering a code on a keypad, entered a small closet. Inside the closet was a console and an array of monitors.

Allen designed this building when she was an Assistant Secretary General. She built in security safe guards to keep planetary leadership safe in case of a riot or some other major problem. It was true she had not anticipated a full out coup, but these safety measures would do the trick. With a few keystrokes the aide was able to engage the program. He was able to see on the monitors that the General was still inside Allen's office. The plan would not work otherwise. On the monitors, he spied Cai responding as heavy barricades fell into place completely closing off the office. Electronic measures were also implemented that prevented communication between the office and the outside world except for a coded security channel that only Allen and her staff had access to.

At the sound of the barricades crashing down, the soldiers accompanying Allen rushed back into the outer office. Two armed security guards stationed near the entrance to the office complex grabbed the Secretary General and rushed her into another secure room. As soon as she was safe inside, she sent a message to every cabinet ministry and the remaining military commanders that a coup had been attempted but that it had been thwarted. She notified them that she was still in charge of the planetary government and plans would be forthcoming to further prevent problems surrounding the coup attempt.

Inside the now cut off and protected office of the Secretary General, General Cai raged at his own staffers but he understood deep down that his attempt failed. What angered him the most was his fear that Marsha Allen would do something to put Earth and every other human in the solar system at risk. Unfortunately, there was nothing to do from inside this new prison.

Hours after receiving no reply to his urgent message to the Negotiator, Commander D'shan was in turmoil. He received communications from the Gathung system concerning the destruction of a large portion of the fleet there. However, he had worries of his own in the Sol system. His own fleet was broken now into two smaller groups. One was still in Earth orbit and his own was in Mars orbit.

He didn't have sufficient battleships to also encircle Titan and neutralize the space hub there. He decided to call in reinforcements. Several members of the secret cabal were in command of reserve fleets not directly involved in the conflict. He ordered one of the fleets to leave their current position near Scree space and jump at once to Sol and take up position near Saturn. He hoped these reinforcements would alleviate any issues with the flawed plan set in place by Negotiator D'iash and enable him to focus on finding a way to invade Earth.

He was not overly concerned with destroying the

Martian colonies. They had no planetary defenses to speak of and his fleet detected no enemy ships nearby. The D'lai intercepted attempts at contacting Earth but those communications failed so he presumed that Mars and even Titan could not coordinate with Earth in defensive planning.

D'shan was still frustrated that he had not heard back from the Negotiator. He sent her information on his own plans as well as the disaster near Gathung'l. It was beyond all understanding why she had not jumped into action herself. He had worked with D'iash for decades and never found her to fail. This new problem fragmented his thoughts. He decided to put that issue away for now and focus on his conquest of the Sol system.

Earlier he received intelligence from the Saturn space hub about some action between an Earth ship and a Gathung ship. The small skirmish was odd because D'shan believed that no Gathung remained in the system. He ordered his spies on the space hub to find out what was going on. He wondered if the interplay there would have any sort of impact on his own actions. He was aware of the secure lab in the hub but his spies had not been able to give him any usable data on what exactly happened there or what was researched.

D'shan suspected the planetary cloak had either been developed there or it played some part in the deployment. Try as he might, he had no luck gaining access to any security camera footage. He made a mental note to execute the spy on the hub if he persisted in failing the D'lai. Failure was not an option and a spy that was no longer useful had no reason to continue existing.

He was startled by an incoming message from Negotiator D'iash.

"Finally!" He said to himself. He punched the icon to open the message.

"Commander D'shan, what is the status of your invasion?"

"Negotiator, we are awaiting reinforcements so that we can take all three planets at the same time."

"Who ordered you to do this?"

"No one did. I took the initiative and acted to rectify *your* failure."

D'iash looked as if she had been slapped. "My failure, Commander? I have very specific plans! Which fleet did you pull?"

D'shan replied, "the fleet from the Scree system."

"Scree? That is a secondary objective and we are going to take that planet once our opening attacks are concluded."

"With all due respect, those ships are just sitting there for no reason other than your vanity."

"Enough, Commander. I am recalling you from your post. You will leave the Sol system and report at once to Cathar Prime."

"That is not going to happen. Your failure to plan this invasion has cost us valuable time. I have the means to finish this and I will do it."

D'shan closed the channel and sent a prerecorded coded message to the other commanders in his cabal. The message was simple – take out *The Spector*. I am assuming command of the D'lai Authority.

Commander D'shan was unaware of the coup attempt on Earth but he fully intended to carry out his plans. D'iash was old and out of touch. It was time for new blood and he was going to get the D'lai a new home no matter what he had to do.

THE D'LAI INVASION OF CATHAR PRIME WAS proceeding at an incredible pace and it would not be

long before the entire planet was under the subjugation of its banished cousins. That was how the situation looked from orbit. While the planet was indeed
burning, something happened to the Cathari people
that the invaders had not expected. They began to
wake up. At first they feared for their lives but soon
self-preservation set in. In small villages and middling
towns and ruined cities, the Cathari people refused to
die without a fight.

Dozens of troop transports landed in various loca-
tions on the planets surface and in almost every
instance, an angry mob of Cathari had been waiting.
They had no weapons to speak of so the resourceful
inhabitants improvised. Some carried pieces of wood,
some had only knives used in food preparation. A few
industrious Cathari used materials readily available
and created makeshift grenades to toss at the unsuspecting D'lai troops. Their numbers were far greater
than those of the D'lai and despite horrific loss of life
the Cathari fought back and started to turn the tide.

In orbit around Cathar Prime, dozens of battleship commanders began to order transports recalled to
spare as many D'lai lives as possible. One by one the
ships lifted off and disappeared from sight. On the
ground, the Cathari sensed a shift and grew bolder in

their insurgency. Two days after the invasion had begun, every D'lai troop that was not killed was back in his barracks in orbit.

Provincial Governor Abiuna was the highest ranking remaining member of the Cathari government to have survived the initial attacks. During the destruction of the capital city, he had been in a summer villa enjoying a well-deserved vacation and was therefore nowhere near any populated region.

Emergency protocols were activated and after some checking and re-checking of surviving government officials, Abiuna was sworn in as Ambassador of Cathar Prime. His first duty was to alert the rest of the Cathari Alliance of the attack to give the other worlds time to enact their own security protocols should the D'lai invade them as well. From what he ascertained from spotty reports, only two other planets, Earth and Gathung'l, were currently under attack by the D'lai.

There was no word on the fate of Earth, but Gathung Interim Leader Bresu Xid broadcast on an alliance secure channel of his planets fight for survival. Abiuna had no doubt that the scrappy Gathung people would do what they could.

His next task was to equip his citizenry. The pacifism of Ambassador Liuna was legendary but it was time for his people to be not only self-reliant but also learn from their own mistakes. The peace of the galaxy was now only an illusion and that illusion cost his planet and the alliance dearly.

"Ambassador, we don't have the manpower to distribute arms to the populace."

"Enough! I don't need excuses, I need solutions. Our people are dying and we must do what we can to prevent that."

"Sir," said the aide, "I will do my best but I don't know what the solution is."

"Let's think this through," said Abiuna, "we have small armories all over the planet. They can't all be destroyed. Our people are not criminals. They will use the weapons with respect."

"Yes, Ambassador."

"Notify any surviving Planetary Guardsman to get those weapons distributed. The D'lai may have abandoned the planet but they are most definitely not done!"

The aide rushed from the room to enact the orders. Abiuna turned to his spouse. "We have something else to do while the citizens arm themselves."

"Yes, Abi? What?"

"We must tell the people. Our secret has been our undoing."

"Abi?"

"You don't know and that is to my shame as much as our dead leaders. Sit down Fio."

Fiola sat down and gestured beside him. "Sit, Abi. Tell me."

Abi sat next to his husband and looked him in the eyes. "Fio, the Cathari and the D'lai, we are one and the same people."

Fiola reacted just as Abiuna knew he would. His heart was much too big and his conscience much too clean for such a secret to not rock him.

"A thousand years ago, our ancestors banished a small sect of citizens in rickety space craft. They refused to embrace our peaceful ways and we sent them off to fend for themselves."

Fiola held his spouses hand in his own. "How long have you known?"

Abiuna sighed, "Ambassador Liuna notified me last winter. She needed to confide and she found me a worthy listener."

The couple held each other in a long embrace. Fiola broke the silence, "we must tell them. We must try to heal what has been done."

"I know, Fio. I know."

Abiuna stood and looked around the small office. His villa was a peaceful place and he knew that with the confession he was about to give, this room would become the center of a firestorm of recriminations and reproach. He also understood this is the right thing to do. He braced himself, and began composing a planetary broadcast. The news would not bring back the dead, but it might help bring about peace. He prayed his ancestors would forgive him.

# CHAPTER 11

Gallagher was moved to a small brig onboard *Atlantis* after his conversation with Secretary General Allen. At least his cell mate, Corey Hodges, was someone he wanted to see as he stood against a bulkhead and avoided the electrified bars of the small cell.

"So, what brings you here?" Gallagher asked.

"Well, it seems our tampering with the cloaks and the disruption beam got us in hot water." Hodges replied.

"You receive any important phone calls while I was away," said Gallagher. "I did."

Hodges sat straighter and smiled.

"Yeah, you're looking at the Major that none other than Secretary General Marsha Allen contacted to *beg* to help."

"Help with what? Fine tuning her air transport's engines?"

"Nah. She asked me to build that cloak for Mars."

"Mars? I guess what they say is true. No one cares about the neighbors."

"Neighbors," said Gallagher. "Which ones? By my count we have *two* neighbors wanting our help."

"Let's compare. Maybe a million people live on Mars."

"Uh huh."

"What's the population of Gathung'l, two or three billion?"

"At least. So do we help our own kind, or those in greatest need?"

"I'm not as concerned about that as I am on figuring out how to escape from this blasted cell so we can at least help *someone*." Hodges said.

"Right, what to do about that?" Gallagher smiled. "I think I might have a plan."

"Then why are we still here?"

"I didn't say it was a *good* plan," said Gallagher.

"Though I do think I could sweet talk our way out of here."

"Sure. This I gotta see."

Gallagher smiled again and then approached the electrified bars carefully to avoid getting shocked into the afterlife.

"Hey, buddy, guard."

The guard looked over at Gallagher with a bored expression. "Yeah?"

"Hey, tell Captain Jimenez that Major Cormac Gallagher needs to talk to him."

"Why would I do that?" The guard started to look back down at his pad.

"Tell him on orders of Secretary General Marsha Allen."

The guard shrugged and punched an icon. After a short conversation Gallagher didn't understand, the guard stood suddenly and moved to the cage.

"It's your lucky day *Major*." The guard entered a code on a keypad and the bars slid away. Gallagher and Hodges both got up to leave. "Not you Hodges. The Captain only wants to talk to Gallagher."

Gallagher looked at Hodges and sat down. "Gee I guess I don't want to talk all that bad."

With a pissed expression, the Guard motioned. "Both of you, c'mon."

Hodges and Gallagher left the cramped cell and followed the guard. They were led to Captain Jimenez's private quarters. Evidently he didn't want to be seen with two felons on the bridge. The guard knocked and after being admitted, he turned and stood in front of the door.

"I'll be right here if you need me Captain."

"Fine," replied Alejandro Jimenez. He stared at the two men. "Well?"

Gallagher hoped his plan would work. He was making everything up as he went. He had no real intention of helping Allen over the Gathung. He did have some ideas on how he might help them both, but everything depended on him convincing Jimenez that he was right.

"Gallagher. You are causing me so much trouble," began Captain Jimenez. "Not only did I have to chase your ship halfway across the solar system, but I had to impound that same ship because you and your buddy here," he motioned toward Hodges, "decided to play hot potato with some highly important tech."

"Captain, I think that..."

"I'm not quite finished, Major." Gallagher

stopped talking. "In addition to all that, now you claim to have some sort of get out of jail free card from Secretary General Allen." He waved a hand in Gallagher's direction. "Speak."

"Captain, that technology was developed by not just Earth. The Gathung had a major role to play. Hell, I flew light years to make it back to this system just to ensure it worked."

"I read about your adventures outside *The Avenger*." When Gallagher appeared puzzled, he laughed. "When we impound ships, we also *read* their logs."

"Gotcha. Anyway, who are we to decide that our *allies* don't deserve the use of the tech they helped develop?"

"That is way about your pay grade and mine also."

"Yeah, so genocide is something we should just sit and let happen?"

"Genocide? That's a big word Major."

"It's what we are allowing if we don't help Gathung'l."

"We only have one cloak left," said Hodges trying to help. "We can't help everyone."

Gallagher shot Hodges an angry look. "Hey, if we can't figure this out what kind of engineers are we?"

Hodges was puzzled. "Figure this out?" He paused for a moment as a thought struck him. "Figure...this...out." He eyed Gallagher who was smiling.

In unison, both men said, *"The Avenger!"*

It was now Captain Jimenez's turn have a puzzled look. Gallagher quickly explained. When they were first developing the planetary cloak, the technology was huge and bulky. They initially configured the cloak on *The Avenger* to act as a satellite would and create the force field necessary for the cloak to work. As their knowledge advanced, they were able to reduce the size of the device needed and reduced it to something that would fit inside the cargo hold. They had never reconfigured *The Avenger* and so, in theory, it would still act in the role of the smaller satellite now orbiting Earth.

"Captain, we need to get that smaller cloak up and running. If we can, we have *two* that can be deployed. We can use the smaller one around Mars..."

"...and *The Avenger* can go defend Gathung'l," said Captain Jimenez. "That's brilliant. Damn but that won't work."

"Why not?

"I don't have authorization from Earth. My orders were to impound *The Avenger*, not set her loose."

"Captain, if we don't, do you really want to be remembered as the Captain that was just following orders or as the Captain that saved an entire *planet?*" Gallagher waited for him to reply.

Jimenez thought for a painfully long moment. "Major, you are *sure* your plan will work?"

"I'm 90% sure."

"Good enough. Let's get to work." Jimenez rose and led Hodges and Gallagher to a science bay. They had to make this work. The fate of billions depended on it.

AFTER THE FAILED COUP ATTEMPT IN LONDON, Secretary General Allen kept a low profile as she continued to monitor the developments of the D'lai attack. As she was reading what seemed like an endless briefing book on cloaking technology, Paula Fister was sitting near her surreptitiously recording the conversation in the room with her phone.

Paula sent her handlers all she gathered on the cloak now enveloping the planet. She had been in prime position to gather the cloaking satellite communication frequencies, how the cloak field operated, and even how it had been deployed. She felt miserable as she betrayed her own people but she had been promised that this technology would not be used against Earth. She had been lied to and assured that it was the Gathung who recruited her.

Now, sitting in the makeshift office of the Secretary General, she had been tasked with recording everything she heard about the coup attempt and what plans were being implemented to protect Mars and other human colonies in the system.

Paula began to suspect something was amiss. For example, why would the Gathung need to know about protection plans for Mars and Titan? How would that be relevant to saving their own civilization. She wanted to come clean and confess but she feared that at this point, they'd simply shoot her and not bother with a trial. So, she kept at her task and hoped for a way out. Inspiration will strike, or so she hoped.

"Colonel, what is the state of the military without Cai?"

"Madam Secretary General, the men and women under my command are horrified at General Cai's actions," replied the Colonel.

"Yes yes I know. What I am trying to find out is,

will there be another attempt? Was this just an opening salvo?"

"Ma'am, General Cai acted on his own. We don't need further chaos added to the invasion."

Allen was not convinced. She tripled her own security and implemented strict lock down procedures to keep everyone away but for those who had an absolute need to be in the room with her.

"We need to know what is happening with that second cloak and Mars. I know we are two separate people now but they are *humans* and we must protect them!"

"Ma'am, with the communications blackout..."

"Fister," said Allen, startling the spy, "brief the Colonel on how we broke the blackout and were able to contact Major Gallagher."

Paula Fister jumped out of her skin when the Secretary General called on her. She had been pondering her own future and how bleak it was.

"Yes, Ma'am. Sir, we used focused lasers pointed at an orbital satellite outside the cloak. That satellite then bounced signals off of other communications arrays first near the Moon and then other planets. Using a very low level radio frequency that is only used in very specific applications..."

"Fister, he doesn't need the technical specs. He needs...never mind I'll do it myself."

The Secretary General and Colonel talked for a time about why and how she communicated and how she had hopes that the second device would be used to protect Mars.

"If I know Prime Minister Arroyo, I know he is seriously worried about his own planet."

"Ma'am," said the Colonel, "we need to have contingency plans in place for our own planet should that cloak fail. We can maybe fight off the D'lai but it will incur mass casualties."

The two leaders conferred on plans that had long been in place since the original Cathari appearance and how Earth had been preparing for a fight ever since. Beside the development of the cloak to keep the xenophobic Earth safe, hundreds of orbital weapons platforms, ground based laser batteries, lunar outposts had all been constructed. The only reason they hadn't been activated was Cai jumping the line with his new toy and hiding the planet first.

"We can't risk firing our ground based defenses through the cloak as it would disrupt the field." Marsha Allen was glad she read the briefing book after all.

An aide approached the pair with a frightened expression on her face.

"Ma'am, Colonel."

The two gaped at her and she stopped mid-sentence. "What is it?

"Ma'am, look." The aide pointed at a pair of monitors that were showing live pictures of where Earth was hiding. On the monitor, the blackness of space was disrupted by blue skies and clouds. To the horror of everyone in the room, a panorama of the planet slowly was revealed. The cloak was coming down. Earth was now visible.

In that instant, alarms began blasting in the room. The invasion had begun in earnest and everyone was running around trying to figure out what to do next. Paula Fister quietly left the office. She understood what happened and it was only a matter of time before someone put the puzzle pieces together and figured out a mole had given the planet away. As she walked, she felt calm and free of emotion. She didn't know precisely where she was going until she found herself near the Liverpool Street Station. She walked calmly as she entered the underground, swiped her card and headed toward her usual line to wait for a train.

Walking behind her, Paula's handler observed and waited. He had been stalking her for days since she revealed the most important piece of technology Earth possessed. He knew at some point, when his masters the D'lai figured out how to use the data, she would do something rash. He thought she'd just turn herself in. It now appeared like she was just going home to her own flat to wait.

Paula stood near the rails as a train approached. Sensing someone behind her, she turned just as her handler gave her a hard shove. Screaming, she fell onto the tracks seconds before the train barreled into the station. People around her shouted and tried to help her but it was too late. The train did not stop and Paula screamed one last time as the train struck her. Her handler faded into the horrified crowd and left the tube station. He had been alerted of an imminent attack and he knew the D'lai would not spare him so he wanted a front row seat to the action. He walked the few blocks from the station to the Finsbury Circus Gardens and sprawled on a manicured lawn under the trees and waited.

THE BATTLE FOR GATHUNG'L HAD BEGUN IN earnest as dozens of battleships and smaller crafts fought it out in the skies over the planet. Overseeing the Gathung allied forces, Interim Leader Xid monitored half a dozen monitors in a conference room on *The Naomor*.

Satellite imagery and ground based sensors displayed flight paths and showed brilliant flashes of lasers as the ships fought. Xid desperately wanted to bring his own ship into the fray, but his naval commanders persuaded him that the planet was best served by remaining cloaked and monitoring the situation.

"No one will benefit from another dead leader," a peeved Admiral had said when Xid ordered the ship to engage a nearby D'lai battleship hammering a much smaller merchant vessel.

"I can't just sit by and watch, Admiral!" Xid protested. "My people are dying."

"Many *will* die Sir, that is the nature of battle. These people need you!"

Bresu Xid acquiesced and ordered his ship to stand down. Ensconced in this room full of displays, Xid and his military commanders gave constant orders and updates to ships and ground based defenses. The

D'lai were a very tough adversary but the Gathung learned from the occupation and employed guerrilla tactics the D'lai did not expect.

A favorite trick of some of the less battle ready Gathung allied ships was to sneak in close to a D'lai battleship while remaining cloaked. Firing while cloaked was not possible, but it could move into a much closer range where its weapons would do the most damage. The toughened armor on the D'lai battleships was strong but not invincible. The closer a laser turret was, the more damage and less dissipation of the beam there was.

The battle had been raging for several hours. So far twenty Gathung ships had been destroyed while less than ten D'lai battleships had been. At this rate, the Gathung would be out of options in less than ten hours. Xid and his aides racked their brains for ways to forestall the inevitable. Even the massive debris field surrounding the planet would not hold off the invaders forever. Eventually, once the Gathung lost the space battle, the D'lai would take their time and clean up the billions of small particles in orbit.

Xid sent another communication blast begging for assistance. He hoped that planets like Scree or even the more distant Earth might send reinforcements. He had no idea that Earth was in a battle for its own survival and that Scree abandoned the alliance all together in an attempt to save itself from a future invasion.

FLEEING THE CATHAR SYSTEM AND EN ROUTE TO Scree, *The Manchester* and its captain Zea Windrow received news of the fighting over Gathung'l and the desperate attempt by Earth to cloak the planet. Her ship was too small to be of much use in a space battle and its limited weapons were purely defensive.

Zea agonized over how to help. A smuggler by trade, she didn't relish the idea of choosing sides, but she also liked the status quo that enabled her profession. The attacking aliens threaten to upend that environment and that angered her.

Her crew captured whatever data available on the opening salvo of the Cathar Prime battle but she escaped without detection. Now, in the middle of nowhere, she hoped she had time to catch her breath and plan her next moves. Flying under cloak as always, she assumed she was as safe as possible so she decided to head to her small bunk and catch some sleep.

As she entered the cramped quarters she allowed herself, a message pinged on her small desk. Opening the message, she saw another desperate plea from Gathung'l. It saddened her because she really had no way of helping those desperate people other than hopes and prayers. Zea was about to crawl into her bunk when inspiration hit her.

One of the tricks of her trade was the ability to sneak into tense situations. There was no doubt the situation around Gathung'l was utterly desperate, but she wondered if she might sneak up close to the D'lai fleet and disrupt it somehow. In the past, when in a tight spot, she learned how to use her limited technology to disrupt a larger ships lasers, sensors, communications, everything. A massive burst of radiation did the trick and helped her escape more times than she cared to remember.

Zea doubted that the Gathung had ever had to resort to such tactics and they probably had never figured out the immense bursts of radiation, the kind a ship that was about to enter FTL produced, could create such havoc. The trick, of course, was to not jump into faster than light speed. That would tear any ship apart if it was too close to a planet or gravity well. However, aborting the jump at the last second still had the benefit of the massive burst.

She ran back to her bridge and ordered her crew to set a course to Gathung'l. Out here there was no reason to not jump immediately. She sat in her command chair and mashed a communications icon on her display, trying to raise anyone in the Gathung fleet that would listen.

After a few desperate attempts, she got in touch with a low level flunky on board a ship called *The Naomor*. It sounded like an important ship so she kept pressing her point.

"As I have said many times, I am not aligned with Gathung'l or any other planet. I have an idea on how to help and my ship is en route."

"You will have to keep this channel clear Ma'am. We have other priorities..."

"So saving your necks isn't one of them? Let me talk to your superior."

"As I also explained, without clearance and proper ID, we can't continue having this conversation. We are fighting for our lives out here," said the communications officer.

"Fine. I'll just do it myself."

Zea clicked off and checked the chronometer. *The Manchester* would arrive in Gathung'l space in less than six hours. That gave her time to get a few hours sleep and to prep her crew for the dangerous maneuvers she planned.

She hoped she was in time to do any good in the battle. She had a lot of crimes to atone for so in some small way her help made her feel like she was contributing at least a small part that might save some lives. Back in her bunk, she set an alarm and closed her eyes and dreamed of more peaceful days.

HODGES AND GALLAGHER WORKED AS HARD AND as fast as possible on the incomplete cloak. They found enough spare parts that they were able to replicate some of the core functions of the prototype now protecting Earth. There would be no time to test this device but Gallagher felt sure it would do the trick.

A crew member ran into the ante room of the clean room the men were toiling in. Activating the intercom, he frantically relayed the news that Earth's cloak had fallen. Gallagher ran to a panel in the corner of the room to check the status of the orbiting prototype.

"Damn, the D'lai are disrupting the shield harmonics of the cloak. The cloak is still active but it is letting visible light escape."

Hodges walked over and checked a few screens for himself.

"Yeah, and to make matters worse, if those harmonics are not restored in time, the entire field will fall and not only will Earth be visible, it will be vulnerable."

The cloak around Earth was indeed allowing visible light to penetrate, but ship based sensors still did not target the planet nor would communications make it through the shielding. However, if the harmonics failed, the whole system would collapse and the D'lai could proceed with their invasion of the planet.

"Hodges, get back to the device and finish up. I'll look at the harmonics and the jamming frequencies being sent by the D'lai and see if I can find a workaround."

Hodges nodded and returned to the task at hand. Modifying the cloak around Earth might be possible but he had to also make this device work as well. The

D'lai would not be satisfied to just take Earth. They would want to crush humanity.

An hour later, Gallagher rubbed his eyes. Staring at specifications and data readouts was hard on the eyes and he wasn't getting any younger. He worked out a few possible solutions but he wanted to make sure that whatever he tried didn't make things worse and bring the whole field down. Hodges had just about finished the new cloaking device and so together the two men programmed scenarios and let the computer simulate each of the proposed solutions.

One by one, each of Gallagher's ideas fizzled as the cloaking field either dissipated or had no effect at all. He was about to give up when Hodges laughed and pointed at the screen.

"Buddy, you've been at this too long. You're missing something in these equations."

Gallagher frowned and checked the data. "I don't see... wait...," he slapped his forehead. The problem that has plagued many mathematicians in history also hit him. He used a + sign when he meant to use a −. Gallagher quickly re-input the data into the computer and let the scenarios run out again. The very first scenario was reported as successful. Taking no chances, he let each of them run out, and out of seven ideas, five of them worked.

Gallagher raced out of the clean room with Hodges at his heels. He barged onto the bridge of *Atlantis* just as Captain Jimenez was lifting a cup of tea to his lips. He dropped the cup as Gallagher and Hodges ran in spilling hot tea over his clean uniform. He cursed and stood, facing the two men.

"What is the meaning of..."

"No time to waste Captain. We have a fix to the cloak around Earth. We have to move in there. I can't program the satellite from this distance. We have to be within ten kilometers."

"That is doable," said Captain Jimenez.

"One problem, Captain," Hodges said, "we can't be cloaked when we do it."

Captain Jimenez frowned as the realization struck him. To save the planet, he might also have to sacrifice the lives of his own crew.

"What about the cloaking of Mars and Titan?"

"We can meet up with *The Avenger* on the way and transfer the device. We'll need her to act as the cloak for one of the two."

Captain Jimenez gave the necessary orders. In a few hours they would rendezvous with *The Avenger*.

The plan was to have Captain Ziqna deploy the smaller cloak around Titan and then to travel at all available speed to Mars and use *The Avenger* to protect Mars. Then, *Atlantis* would head to Earth and work to repair the cloak there.

When the two ships finally met up, Jimenez dispatched a small shuttle with the cloak to *The Avenger*. Hodges went with the cloak to deploy the satellite and then rig the larger ship. No one on Ziqna's ship had the technical skills to do this on their own, and Jimenez secretly didn't trust that Ziqna would not steal the device for his own home.

"Hodges, if you even suspect that *The Avenger* is leaving the system, do whatever you can to stop it!" Jimenez ordered Hodges. Even though Hodges had no military rank, he trusted that he would do the right thing. Hodges agreed. He served aboard *The Avenger* for a long time so he trusted that Ziqna would do right. Besides, the cloak they built was not large enough to protect the much larger Gathung'l. That planet was larger by 20% than Earth. The original prototype had been too small as it was and barely covered Earth.

After some final instructions and communications, the ships parted and headed to their destinations. Down in a temporary office, Gallagher continued to fine tune the program he would send to the cloak around Earth. He only had a few hours and this could be a one time shot. If the D'lai targeted *Atlantis,* all would be lost.

# CHAPTER 12

Negotiator D'iash was not about to give up command of the D'lai Authority to that interloper D'shan. She worked for decades to get this attack off the ground and she was going to see it through. Cathar Prime was going to be a long fight but she felt confident that with enough time and a continuation of the attack plans, the D'lai would prevail.

She decided to hand off local command to a local commander and take her own ship to the Gathung system to confront D'shan in person. She learned all about the cabal of commanders he assembled. If D'shan thought she was stupid or out of touch, he would be very surprised to find out that D'iash had a few tricks up her ancient sleeve as well.

The truth was, she didn't really know about the cabal until her security agents onboard *The Spector* rooted out the traitor that helped Gallagher to escape. D'lai methods of torture are quite effective and the villain gave up everything he remembered about the subversive plans by D'shan and his ilk. She had been enraged to find that thirty percent of her battleship commanders had been secretly plotting to overthrow her and disrupt her long laid plans. Once her security squeezed every ounce of information out of the traitor, they blew him out of an airlock. With any luck the traitor's body would burn up in the Cathari atmosphere.

Long term thinking was one of D'iash's strengths. She planned long ago for any kind of attempt at a coup. Each battleship had a redundant command structure that would work just fine if the local commander was out of action. She gave a simple pre-programmed command and every commander on every ship in all three fleets was arrested and locked in their own quarters. D'iash intended to make an example out of all of them to prove to her troops and naval forces that she was in command.

Commander D'shan had been in a meeting with fellow cabal commanders when the order was given. He was mid-sentence when security burst into the conference room. On each screen of each cabal member, a similar action was taking place. D'shan was escorted not to his quarters, but to the bridge of his ship. When he arrived, he found his bridge officers lined up against the bulkheads, watching. On a view screen he saw the smiling face of Negotiator Ret D'iash.

"Commander D'shan," she began. "I hope you weren't too busy."

"What is the meaning of this, Negotiator."

"Don't pretend you don't know, D'shan. I know all about your little cabal and I have crushed it." She pointed to a screen behind her. "Even now each of your friends has been arrested and their crews are watching as they are put to death."

D'shan glared as his fellow commanders were gunned down or blown out of airlocks. One crew even used a primitive sword and decapitated their commander. D'shan was horrified and feared his own fate.

D'iash turned back from the monitor and once

again faced D'shan. "Don't worry, Commander. Your fate is already decided."

"You are a worthless leader who has led us into disaster, D'iash." He didn't bother to use her honorific as he addressed the Negotiator. "We will fail if we follow your plans."

D'iash laughed and pressed a key on her panel. On D'shan's ship, a countdown timer began counting backwards from 10. D'shan realized in sudden horror that D'iash was going to kill not only him, she was going to destroy his entire ship.

9...8...7...

"Goodbye traitor." D'iash ended the communication. D'shan faced his doomed crew.

6...5...4...

They turned their backs to him in unison and bowed their heads.

3...2...1...

Fire and debris ripped through the ship as the vacuum of space rushed in, imploding the hull and killing the entire crew.

After she closed the connection, D'iash turned her attention back to the work at hand. Her data analysts and scientists found a useful hack that they were able to implement to degrade the cloak surrounding Earth. She was assured that even though they would still not directly attack the planet, they would see it and the cloak would fail within six to eight hours. At that point, the D'lai fleet would bombard the planet and implement the conquest protocols designed specifically for the humans.

Each of the three worlds under invasion had different requirements and D'iash fine-tuned those plans and anticipated as much as possible. Cathar Prime was hers. Gathung'l would fall soon. Now it was time for Earth. Those smug humans had no idea what was in store for them.

Ret D'iash badly misjudged human tenacity.

WITH THE D'LAI STILL IN ORBIT AND CONSTANTLY threatening and bombarding the planet, Ambassador Abiuna established a temporary headquarters and was in constant contact with ground forces and surviving regional leaders. Hours earlier he sent a broadcast to every available Cathari device capable of receiving communications. He informed his people of their centuries old shame and reminded them of the generosity of their own civilization. He asked for collective forgiveness for the sins of their ancestors and their leaders.

The Cathari people were shaken by the revelations but not surprised. Ancient allegories still taught in religious houses alluded to an historic exodus and shame. Creation stories taught of a divided people who conquered the stars. Every Cathari knew these stories though few took them as more than a good story to tell. Now, with the revelation of Ambassador Abiuna, those inhabitants that were not fighting gathered in groups. They prayed to their gods, chanted ancient prayers, and attempted to sooth their own souls.

Abiuna had not expected a spiritual re-awaking of his people but he hoped that by knowing their past, they might now confront their present. Recognizing the incalculable pain of the D'lai at having been exiled from their home, he hoped the Cathari would be able to negotiate peace from the D'lai. He didn't expect it to work, but he hoped that their leaders would be open to listening. The peaceful ideals of the Cathari Alliance would be the tool that helps save themselves.

The Ambassador sent overtures of peace to the orbiting ships. In his message he explained the deep shame of the Cathari, and his hopes that the two peoples should come together in unity. He invited the D'lai to return home and make their lives among their cousins.

His answer from the D'lai and Negotiator D'iash came back swiftly and with such ferocity it almost cracked the planet. In orbit, all remaining ships in the D'lai fleet set as their target the small villa where the communications originated from. Firing in near unison, the concentrated power of the destructive blasts sent shock waves that destroyed millions of square miles around Abiuna and Fiola's villa. The force of the blast triggered an earthquake and killed thousands of ordinary Cathari who gathered nearby to pray.

In orbit, Negotiator D'iash thought she had been patient enough. She ordered every troop transport on every ship to land on the planet. Every ship in orbit was directed to bombard the ground. Any gathering of Cathari sensors detected would be blasted. She may very well leave the planet in ruins, but she was not going to move on without complete and total domination. It was time to end the Cathari and her foolish alliance. It was time to end this entire war once and for all.

D'iash ordered every fleet at her disposal to gather in one of the three systems. If she had to, she'd find her people a new home world. Her brush with the coup and the utterly offensive apology from the Cathari moved her beyond her original planning. She was going to defeat the three worlds if it was the very last thing she did. She smiled. The end was in sight – or so she thought.

THE MANCHESTER ARRIVED IN THE GATHUNG system hours after Zea attempted to convince anyone who would listen of her plan. She presumed that with everything going on, a crazy person with a crazy idea might not be a top priority for ship commanders and planetary leaders.

Nevertheless, she coordinated a tight plan with her crew and she intended to implement it. She ordered her ship to come in close to Gathung'l to map out the best place to employ her strategy. She was aghast at the immense battle taking place over the planet. From her vantage point, she counted hundreds of ships flying around each other, firing, evading, blowing up.

The planet itself was blurred by the sheer vastness of the debris field orbiting it. "I wouldn't want to try to land down there," she thought to herself. She examined all the available data and a clear pattern soon emerged. Of all the ships fighting, two appeared to be hanging back from the fray. One of the ships she recognized as being *Naomor* so the other must be the D'lai command ship.

"Helm, get us in as close as you can to that big destroyer."

Navigating the various ships and floating debris field proved tricky, but after some delicate maneuvering, her navigator got within a kilometer of the enormous destroyer.

"Easy, easy," urged Zea. "Tactical, are our cloaks still active?"

"Yes Captain," came the reply.

"Good. Navigator, stop the ship and execute the pre-programmed FTL jump command."

Zea hoped there were no errors in the calculations. If the FTL jump could not be aborted, the gravity of Gathung'l and the orbiting space craft would rip her ship into pieces.

She crossed her fingers as the navigator confirmed her orders. Counting down, everyone braced themselves. When the timer hit zero, alert klaxons blared on the bridge as the computer recognized the aborted FTL jump and assumed there was an imminent threat.

Zea prepared herself mentally for the alarms but they still shocked her and caused her heart to skip a few beats. She looked at her navigator who confirmed that the ship had not jumped and looked at her displays. Zea didn't expect to see results immediately and she was surprised to see firing from D'lai ships was halting all over the battlefield.

"I didn't expect *that* result," she said aloud to anyone within earshot.

Without realizing it, the radiation burst her ship sent after the aborted FTL jump had the effect of disrupting the internal computer networks of every D'lai ship in orbit. The D'lai had not hardened their ships against such a burst because they used a very different technology to create the FTL jump. A jump for a D'lai ship produced only negligible radiation. They had not accounted for a ship purposely trying to FTL jump so close to a planet – or to one of their own ships.

Zea and her crew watched in amazement as, one by one, D'lai ships spiraled toward the planet. The ships now lacked navigation through the complicated battlefield and were unable to maintain enough orbital speed to avoid the gravity of Gathung'l. Over the course of the next hour as Gathung allied ships attacked the disabled D'lai battleships, space ship after space ship fell into the gravity of the planet and was chewed up in the destructive orbiting debris field.

"Captain, we have an incoming transmission from *The Naomor*."

"Put it on speaker."

"This is Interim Leader Bresu Xid to the Captain of unidentified Earth ship."

"Leader Xid, this is Captain Zea Windrow of *The Manchester*."

"Captain Window, what did you do?"

The astonishment in Xid's voice could not be hidden despite his heavy Gathungi accent and natural guttural voice.

"Sir, we used the radiation spike from an aborted FTL jump. Um... we didn't know it would have such an effect. I was only trying to disrupt their communications."

Xid started to laugh. "That is funny Windrow. Tell me, you didn't perhaps learn that trick in... um... less than legal ways?"

Zea laughed in return. "Who'd have thought a smuggler would come in handy in a planetary battle!"

Both of them laughed and then spoke at length. Xid wanted to alert everyone of the methods that had been employed that disabled the D'lai fleet. Windrow didn't see why it couldn't be replicated but she also understood that most commanders wouldn't risk their entire crew for such a risky move.

Xid closed the channel and Zea contemplated their next move.

"You know, I think after this I might just go straight. I bet they can use a good pilot or two to clean up this place."

On the D'lai destroyer, the crew and Captain faced the planet as their ship was drawn inevitably down. He sent a communications blast to other D'lai ships to warn of this new trick. The commander looked on in horror as the planet drew closer. He realized that if this trick were employed anywhere else, the D'lai were finished. He only hoped as death took him that this was not all a wasted effort.

ATLANTIS APPROACHED THE CLOAKING SATELLITE orbiting Earth. When they were within range, Captain Jimenez ordered the cloak to be disabled as Gallagher frantically sent the series of commands he programmed to the failing device.

"Rebooting the satellite now," confirmed Gallagher. He waited in agony as the cloak shut down and then restarted.

"How long will this take Major?"

"Sir, it should take no more than five minutes for systems to regain functionality."

"Five minutes we sit here unprotected." Jimenez said. "Tactical, what is the distance to any D'lai vessel?"

"Sir, none within firing range," said the officer. "Correction, none within firing range but I show three battleships closing in on us. They will be within firing range in... six minutes."

"Cutting it a little close Major! Let's get this thing going!"

"Captain, it will take as long as it takes." Gallagher said in as even a tone as he could manage, even though on the inside he was twisted with nervous energy.

"Get the cloak on standby, be ready to re-engage it on my command."

The cloak would take thirty seconds to cycle before it could be engaged. Add that to the five minutes it would take to restart the cloaking satellite, and there was a very short window of time left.

Jimenez bounced his leg up and down in nervousness as he waited. He was prepared to sacrifice himself to protect his home world but he didn't relish the idea of also killing his own crew.

"Gallagher..."

"Hold on Captain."

Jimenez began composing in his head a message he would send to his crew if the D'lai intercepted them before they could re-engage their own cloak. He then thought of his life back on Earth and his family. He knew this cloak was the only way for him to protect them from the murderous D'lai. If he failed, billions on Earth would perish.

"Captain, we have an incoming message from... Gathung'l."

Jimenez was open to a minor distraction. By his estimation they had less than two minutes until the satellite rebooted.

"Put it on," ordered the Captain.

"This is Zea Windrow of *The Manchester*. I have discovered a method to disable all D'lai ships. Using an aborted FTL jump, the radiation spike that it causes disrupts the computer networks aboard their vessels, disabling them. Every D'lai ship in orbit around Gathung'l has been completely destroyed and the planet is now safe. Use this information as you will. I am transmitting precise specs on this communication."

The channel closed and Jimenez whistled loudly at the information. He turned to his Science officer, "process that data and see if it is usable. Find out if it's for real or not."

He turned to Gallagher, "status, Major."

"The satellite's systems are operational. I am re-engaging the cloak."

Jimenez observed from a window as the planet below slowly faded into non-existence. The repair worked. He turned to tactical.

"Tactical..."

"Our cloak is re-engaged."

Jimenez almost collapsed with relief into his command chair. Now all he had to worry about was what was happening with *The Avenger* and the remaining cloaking abilities to protect the rest of humanity in the system.

He was about to stand when the deck tilted sideways and artificial gravity was temporarily lost. The ship shuddered as the nearby D'lai ship managed to get off a salvo at his ship just before the cloak re-engaged.

"Battle stations!"

"Cloak is off-line. Hull armor is offline. I read hull buckling on multiple decks."

"Do we have power, can we evade?"

"Negative. All systems not responding."

"Tactical...I need..."

"Captain, nothing is responding. I believe we have only minutes before the ship is destroyed."

Another blast from the attacking ship threw everyone off their feet.

"All hands abandon ship! All hands abandon ship!"

Everyone ran for the exits except for Captain Jimenez who sat down and waited.

He believed that a captain should go down with his ship. As a hundred escape pods rocketed away from the doomed *Atlantis*, he sang a Welsh lullaby to himself that his mother sang when he was a young boy.

*Huna blentyn ar fy mynwes,* (Sleep child upon my bosom,)

*Clyd a chynnes ydyw hon;* (it is cozy and warm)

*Breichiau mam sy'n dynn amdanat,* (Mothers arms are tight around you)

*Cariad mam sy dan fy mron;* (a Mother's love is in my breast)

*Ni chaiff dim amharu'th gyntun,* (nothing shall disturb your slumber)

THE NEGOTIATOR RAGED AT HER CREW ABOUT the disasters unfolding in Gathung and Earth space. Her *entire* fleet around Gathung'l was *gone!* Earth was once again under a cloak. Her carefully laid out plan was falling to pieces around her.

To make matters worse, her ship intercepted the message from *The Manchester* letting anyone who heard it know precisely how to kill any D'lai ship they came into contact with.

D'iash could not believe that something as simple as an aborted FTL jump would ruin everything! How had they overlooked a detail like that? If she got out of this mess alive heads would roll. Perhaps no one would have anticipated the very different effects of FTL jumps between civilizations, but that didn't matter. What mattered now was rescuing as much of the plan as possible.

On her orders, her fleet around Cathar Prime prepared to land on the planet. Every orbiting battleship was capable of making a safe descent through a planet's atmosphere without burning up. That was one detail at least that D'iash planned for. Her ground troops had been efficient at mopping up any remaining resistance among the Cathari. The last ditch plan was to settle on the planet and make this the home of her remaining civilization. If she had to commit genocide to do it, well it served the Cathari right for banishing her people in the first place.

As *The Spector* made its way down to the surface, D'iash recalled the remaining fleets in the Sol system, the Scree system, and everywhere else she sent rein-forcements to wait further commands. All D'lai were ordered to Cathar Prime. They would at least have *this* world as their new home.

The aged Negotiator sensed her age as she walked down the exceptionally long corridors of her flagship. The tremors in her legs made her feel unsteady but she was determined not to need the assistance of anyone as she slowly walked.

She made it within a few feet of her quarters when she collapsed. Unable to lift herself up, she laid on the floor and fumed at her weakness. She understood this illness would eventually kill her, but she had no wish to appear weak, especially after such a phenomenal failure of her plan to take all *three* worlds and not just this pitiful backwater. She bombarded it so hard she didn't even know if there was anything left to salvage or rule over.

A passing crewman saw her laying on the floor of the corridor and helped her to her bed. Once there, he placed what she thought was a soothing hand on her chest. D'iash quickly realized it was not an attempt to soothe her at all. This crew member was pressing down on her throat. He was choking her. D'iash was too feeble and weak to provide much resistance. As the life ebbed out of her frail body, she raged against the impending death. She had so much she still needed to do. Her eyes flashed in both horror and pain as her attacker mercilessly squeezed so hard he ruptured her vocal cords. The last sensation Negotiator Ret D'iash felt was the agonizing pain and then nothing at all. The crew member smiled as he exited her quarters. D'iash may have thought she rooted out the cabal that threatened her rule, but she had only taken out the leadership. The rank and file was still very much active. Now that the Negotiator was dead, they might begin in earnest. The war may have been lost, but the galaxy had not heard the last of the D'lai.

On Mars, Secretary General Marsha Allen arrived with full fanfare in the grand dome erected to hold the interplanetary summit that had been arranged after the D'lai conquest failed. Cathar Prime may be under their subjugation, but if Allen had her way, the remaining civilizations in the Cathari Alliance and Earth would find a way to free their friends.

Second Dictator Bresu Xid, recently confirmed as planetary leader of Gathung'l, was already waiting and chatting with Martian Prime Minister Arroyo when Allen arrived. Smiling, he turned to face her and shocked her when he embraced her in human fashion. Allen had been prepared by her protocol office not to touch the Leader for fear of sparking a diplomatic incident. Xid had been given a very similar briefing but he decided to do away with the protocol and show his affection.

After the Cathari had been conquered by the D'lai, Earth lowered its planetary cloak and sent emissaries to Gathung'l in an attempt at brokering peace. Allen was devastated at the actions of former General Cai and intended to make things right with her allies. She thought it was only right that the two worlds shared the technology they worked on together. Allen was ashamed that her planet hid while Cathar Prime and Gathung'l had to fight it out with the D'lai.

Leader Xid inherently understood why General Cai acted as he had. If the roles had been reversed, he felt sure he would have done much the same thing. Nevertheless, he appreciated the overtures from Earth and in return for a show of friendship, he asked Earth to help him clean up the orbital mess the Gathung created to defend their home.

Allen quickly agreed. It took six weeks to remove enough of the matter from orbit before it was deemed safe for ships to travel to and from the planet. The first ship to land was *Naomor*. Xid wanted to be among his people and rejoice with them. They defeated the D'lai in spectacular fashion and their civilization's pride was on full display.

The three worlds, Earth, Mars, and Gathung'l, agreed to a joint summit on Mars exactly three months after the D'lai invasion ended. Ships thought this region of the galaxy, whenever encountering a D'lai ship, used the FTL jump trick to destroy it. All told, half the D'lai naval fleet had been destroyed and the remaining half was either in hiding on Cathar Prime or off somewhere else. The three worlds knew they had to be diligent and not let down their guard. They would not repeat the mistakes of the Cathari Alliance and use only peace as the method of building community.

Each leader, Allen, Xid, and Arroyo, pledged mutual aid to each other and promised to share their technology. Xid was impressed at what the Martians had done and offered to assist in the terraforming of the planet. Allen marveled at the Gathung spirit and promised to visit Gathung'l just as soon as she could.

At the conclusion of the summit, the three leaders gathered in an atrium under the weak Martian sun. The room was filled with diplomats, military officials, civilian leaders, scientists, and even ordinary citizens from all three worlds. Each being present portrayed their cultures in their dress, their stature, and most of all, by the fact that they were all together, mingled and engaging as equals. Gallagher, Hodges and Windrow smiled from the foot of the dais where the planetary leaders were now being seated. One by one, Xid, Allen, and Arroyo signed the treaty establishing a new Alliance. The Three Worlds Alliance.

Despite the best efforts of the D'lai and even the Cathari, something remarkable happened on Mars that day. Peace broke out. Three planets erupted in cheers. The day would come that would test this new alliance, but it was time for celebrations and toasts. The new trio of worlds, united as one, rejoiced.

# EPILOGUE

**T**wenty years after the historic signing of the Three Worlds Alliance, stirrings and whispers of a growing threat spread on the lips of those who happened to pass near Cathar Prime. The planet had grown quiet and had been almost forgotten as the peace of the Three Worlds spread. Scree and dozens of other civilizations had joined hands in renewed friendship. Their joy of survival had become the bliss of forgetfulness. No one spoke of the D'lai. The dreams of the masses were no longer haunted by their rage. The name no longer induced primal fear, and yet, no one ever completely forgot them.

As memories faded and civilizations expanded,

the D'lai waited. Their ancient rage had only been tempered in defeat. They would not move on until they had gained what they believed they had lost. A new Negotiator had risen from the ashes of the fallen D'lai Authority. Cathar Prime had submitted itself to its new overlords and working now as one, they forged new weapons, new methods of conquest and a vast new fleet. The D'lai would not be silenced forever, and in time, they would rise from the ashes of their self-imposed exile.

On Earth, Secretary General Cormac Gallagher watched the overhead display of fireworks celebrating the twentieth anniversary of the Alliance. Standing shoulder to shoulder with the Third Dictator of Gath-ung'l and the Martian Prime Minister, he was amazed at all that had been accomplished in such a short time. Earth, Gathung'l, and Mars were permanently shrouded in planetary cloaks and they believed they were safe from invasion and the devastation that it caused. Their technology had grown by leaps and bounds and yet they would always keep a watchful eye on the stars. If the D'lai had been a force to be reckoned with, there must be others out there who wished harm on peaceful worlds.

Deep in the pit of his stomach, Gallagher understood that the D'lai and civilizations like them were a constant threat and he desperately wanted to ensure that his home would be safe. Little did he know that in time, the threat from the D'lai would once again envelop the known galaxy and every world that stood in their path would burn.

# CHAPTER 1

*Cathar Prime – The Present*

The Negotiator sat in the semi-darkened room, waiting for the arrival of The Emissary. Decades earlier the D'lai had been vanquished in the skies above Gathung'l and Earth. The shame and failure of Negotiator Ret D'iash left an immutable scar upon the D'lai consciousness. Those few survivors who remained, fled to the scorched and ruined planet Cathar Prime in a desperate bid to find a shred of peace. In systems all over the Orion Arm, countless D'lai ships had been disabled and destroyed, thanks to the discovery of smuggler Zea Windrow. Her FTL jump trick sent many thousands of D'lai to their doom in the stars they still believed theirs to rule.

Now, alone and virtually homeless, the D'lai remnant waited and planned for their triumphant return. It took years, but they rebuilt Cathar Prime in their own image. Any native Cathari who dared to defy their right to rule the scarred planet was banished into space. The D'lai meted out the same cruelty the Cathari imposed upon them centuries ago.

Cathar Prime had once been home to the vast Cathari Alliance, and boasted beautiful cities and graceful countryside. The Alliance crumbled after the war, leaving Earth and its allies to form the Three Worlds Alliance in its place. Now, twenty years since the violent conquest of the Cathar Prime, no corner of this once majestic planet was free of devastation. The planet's former capital city had never been rebuilt. The D'lai cruelly left its smoldering remains as a memorial, and a reminder, for the ordinary Cathari of their enduring shame, and crushing defeat. With time, smaller cities slowly sprang up out of the ruins, and the D'lai overlords and Cathari survivors now maintained an uneasy peace.

Among the successors of the D'lai, a new Negotiator arose. He studied under the disgraced Ret

D'iash, and expanded upon her cruel but cunning methods of conquest, command, and fear. Negotiator Brik Zat'ol had been aboard *The Spector* when the final battle was lost. He witnessed first-hand the barbarity of D'iash in not only implementing her conquest plans, but in how she dealt with the secretive cabal of Commanders that attempted to overthrow her rule. Zat'ol, then a junior officer on board *The Spector,* had himself been recruited to the cabal and worked to undermine her authority. Despite this, his greatest accomplishment in the final battle did not shower him in glory, but it did bring him personal pride. As he was traveling down a corridor of the ship, he stumbled upon the ill Negotiator outside her quarters, and after helping her inside, he murdered her with his bare hands. The dark memory of that moment still brought him undiluted pleasure.

Now he sat in this poorly lit room, awaiting the visit of an Emissary from the ancient Umawei Empire. Anticipation of the meeting thrilled him. Centuries in the past, when the D'lai had been expelled from Cathar Prime by a religious sect called the Däk'in, the D'lai encountered the remnants of the Umawei Empire in a system they called Ryi Bruai. Awed by the mega structures left by these mysterious aliens, the D'lai believed they found the origins of life on their planet.

The ancient Cathari long ago reasoned that a superior race of beings must have seeded all the habitable planets in this region of space with the building blocks of life. Their reasoning was simple. As they explored their region of the galaxy, they discovered that far too many species resembled each other in appearance and basic anatomy. A coincidence of nature? Probably not. They believed that if they could find the source, they could bring about a true galactic peace. The D'lai, on the other hand, held very different ideas around the source. They maintained that knowledge and possession of this seeding technology, if it fell into the right hands, would be an unstoppable source of unlimited power.

In an effort to prove their early theories of this ancient civilization, the Cathari sought them out with their vigorous exploration of nearby stars. As they explored, they encountered planets teeming with life comparable to their own. It grieved them, however, that only a few planets had advanced civilizations capable of space flight. Their travels through the stars increased their belief in the ancient aliens, however, they also began to realize that what they sought was a darker, more menacing, and immensely powerful civilization. They found scattered relics of this extinct culture in multiple systems, but none as enormous as those the D'lai encountered much later, after the schism.

As they fled Cathar Prime, the D'lai ran across an entire star system filled with planet and star-sized constructions. The discovery thrilled the D'lai, and enabled them to greatly advance their own technological prowess. D'lai leaders recognized that if they might ever recover from the horror of war and banishment, they needed superior knowledge. The Umawei Empire's remnants provided that ability. Unfortunately, due to the circumstances of their exile, the ancient D'lai never fully assimilated the abandoned Umawei technology. Their search for a home far outweighed the thrilling discovery. Centuries later, Zat'ol aimed to correct that early blunder. The D'lai would rise from the ashes of their failures, and assert their rightful place as masters of the galaxy.

As Zat'ol pondered the history of his people, something interrupted him. An aide approached and bowed. The Emissary had arrived.

www.ingramcontent.com/pod-product-compliance
Lightning Source LLC
Chambersburg PA
CBHW060354260626
47160CB00006B/2313